THE DUMB HOUSE

John Burnside was born in 1955 and now lives in Fife.
He has published six collections of poetry, the most
recent being *A Normal Skin*, and has received a number
of awards, including the Geoffrey Faber Memorial Prize.
He was selected as one of the twenty New Generation
Poets in 1994. *The Dumb House* is his first novel.

By the same author

THE HOOP
COMMON KNOWLEDGE
FEAST DAYS
THE MYTH OF THE TWIN
SWIMMING IN THE FLOOD
A NORMAL SKIN

THE DUMB HOUSE

A Chamber Novel

JOHN BURNSIDE

Jonathan Cape
London

First published 1997

1 3 5 7 9 10 8 6 4 2

© John Burnside 1997

John Burnside has asserted his right
under the Copyright, Designs and Patents Act 1988
to be identified as the author of this work

First published in the United Kingdom in 1997 by Jonathan Cape,
Random House, 20 Vauxhall Bridge Road, London SW1V 2SA

Random House Australia (Pty) Limited
20 Alfred Street, Milsons Point, Sydney,
New South Wales 2061, Australia

Random House New Zealand Limited
18 Poland Road, Glenfield,
Auckland 10, New Zealand

Random House South Africa (Pty) Limited
Endulini, 5A Jubilee Road, Parktown 2193, South Africa

Random House UK Limited Reg. No. 954009

A CIP catalogue record for this book is available from the British Library

Papers used by Random House UK Limited are natural,
recyclable products made from wood grown in sustainable forests.
The manufacturing processes conform to the environmental
regulations of the country of origin.

ISBN 0–224–04207–6

Typeset by Palimpsest Book Production Limited,
Polmont, Stirlingshire

Printed and bound in Great Britain
by Mackays of Chatham PLC

I would like to gratefully acknowledge the assistance of the Authors' Foundation in the completion of work on this book.

I am not yet so lost in lexicography, as to forget that words are the daughters of earth, and that things are the sons of heaven. Language is only the instrument of science, and words are but the signs of ideas: I wish, however, that the instruments might be less apt to decay, and that signs might be permanent, like the things which they denote.

Samuel Johnson

part one

karen

No one could say it was my choice to kill the twins, any more than it was my decision to bring them into the world. Each of these events was an inevitability, one thread in the fabric of what might be called destiny, for want of a better word – a thread that neither I nor anyone else could have removed without corrupting the whole design. I chose to perform the laryngotomies, if only to halt their constant singing – if singing is what you would call it – that ululation that permeated my waking hours, and entered my sleep through every crevice of my dreams. At the time, though, I would have said it was a logical act, another step in the research I had begun almost four years before – the single most important experiment that a human being can perform: to find the locus of the soul, the one gift that sets us apart from the animals; to find it, first by an act of deprivation and then, later, by a logical and necessary destruction. It surprised me how easy it was to operate on those two half-realised beings. They existed in a different world: the world of laboratory rats, or the shifting and functionless space of the truly autistic.

That experiment is over now. It was terminated, only in order that it might begin again, in a different form. If I know anything, I know this is the true pattern of our lives: a constant repetition, with small, yet significant variations, unfolding through the years. The experiment with the twins was just one variation on a lifelong theme. If it had been a conventional piece of work, I would be writing up the results; describing, in abstract language, an initial problem, a series of hypotheses and tests, a final outcome. Everything would be clearly stated, in scientific terms. But this was not a conventional piece of work. There is no way to describe this experiment without describing everything that has happened, from the morning I first learned to talk, thirty years ago, to the moment I locked the door of the basement room, leaving the twins inside, silenced now, gazing at one another with those expressions of grieved bewilderment that finally made it impossible for the experiment to continue. I switched on the music before I left, but I still had no way of knowing what it had meant to them during their years of isolation. Outside, I put my eye to the observation grille for a last look; they seemed not to have noticed my departure. Quietly, I left them to digest their poisoned meal, went upstairs to check on Karen, then made a pot of coffee and waited.

It seems odd now, this silence. Perhaps it was what I expected all along; perhaps it was what I wanted. This silence is more than the absence of sound. This is something I have earned: now I understand that, without it, I could not have contemplated this account. I had to know what the end was before I started. Now I can begin at the beginning, with Mother in her fine clothes, coming to my room in the evenings to read me stories, Mother in her pearls and beautiful dresses, one of those exquisite parasites which infect and inhabit their host, without ever going so far as to destroy it entirely – and even, in this case, creating the illusion of a natural symbiosis, a mutual nourishment. It is impossible not to admire such elegance.

Not that I would judge her harshly for that. I loved her as much as it is possible to love anyone. Looking back, I can see her faults. I can be detached, even clinical, in my analysis of our life together; yet, even now, I still love her. As a child, I was stunned by the presence of that marvellous being, that woman who had made of herself an object so beautiful that even she would stop sometimes and wonder at her own reflection in a mirror or a darkened pane of glass. As children, we love who we can. My father was shy with me, difficult, wrapped in a cocoon, always afraid that I would enter somehow, and touch him. I think he was more afraid of me than he was of Mother: he was haunted by a possible betrayal, by seeming to be the one who intruded between us, so he adopted the role Mother had prescribed for him, the role of invisible husband.

At some level, I probably always knew how distant Mother was, even from me. She was always working, like an architect, building a house of stories, treating her life and mine as a piece of fiction. I knew she was engaged in an exercise, an invention in the old sense of the word: everything she did was controlled, every story she told was a ritual. Nothing ever varied, and I admired that. Our relationship resembled that of the priest and the altar boy at Mass: she was the celebrant, I was the witness; our roles and offices were divinely appointed, therefore inevitable. Even now, I suspect she was right: because of her stratagems, our life was ordered. We could avoid intimacy without skulking in our rooms, as my father did; by the use of rituals and stories, she created a neutral ground where we could meet, where everything could be kept under control, and nothing would slip beyond the boundaries we set for ourselves.

When others were present, we were formal, perhaps even cold. It was my father who opened up to guests, telling them stories about his early years in the business, his time in Palestine, his clumsy courtship of my mother, inviting his listeners into a form of collaboration, while she regarded him with a remote,

5

almost contemptuous expression. His favourite story was the one about their first meeting – how, walking a country road, in the summer twilight, he encountered a beautiful young woman with curly brown hair, lugging a parcel along Blackness Lane. He was in uniform at the time. He stopped and offered to help, and that was how they met: a man in uniform, home on leave, visiting a friend from a neighbouring village, and the pretty girl who let him carry her package, then hardly said a word to him all the way home. Mother would listen while he told this story, then interrupt, towards the end.

'It was nothing like that,' she would say to the guests. Then she would turn to my father and say, in seeming mock-annoyance, 'I wish you wouldn't tell such ridiculous stories.'

Mother insisted on my presence at these gatherings; she wanted a witness to my father's folly and I fulfilled the office to the best of my ability, which only made my father more awkward with me later, after the guests had left. At the time, I suspected his stories were true – I even understood his bewilderment – but they failed to meet Mother's standards, not of truth, but of correctness, a standard that might be applied to a piece of fiction, or a portrait. I see now how I resemble her. Sometimes, standing in the kitchen, I look out at the dark, and I see her face, gazing back at me from the shrubbery. It's my own face, but it only takes a minor trick of the light and I see her in myself: the same eyes, the same mouth. It's an easy resemblance to find, but it has taken me till now to see that I also resemble my father – how I am just as weak as he was, and how it was that weakness that caused the experiment with the twins to fail. Something in my spirit is irresolute. Everything should be taken seriously, in the spirit of a game; I should have carried out this experiment with the same unwavering attentiveness that is demanded by a puzzle, or a good story. That is the essence of scientific endeavour. My problem was that I failed to play; I was solemn, rather than serious. I didn't think enough. I failed to translate the intention into the act.

Later, when I went down to the basement, the twins were dead. They lay on the floor near one of the speakers; they were huddled together, embracing one another in a way that reminded me of young monkeys, the way they cling to anything when they are frightened. I waited a long time before I opened the door. I think, even then, that I was afraid of them, afraid they were tricking me in some inexplicable fashion, afraid they were not really dead, but pretending, hoping to catch me unawares. Yet what harm could they have done me? They were small children, after all. I opened the door and crossed to where they lay: they were dead, of course, and it seemed they had died without too much suffering. Certainly their pain would have been minimal, compared to the agonies Lillian had endured, in those few days after they were born. I was glad of that. It seemed appropriate to bury them next to her, in the iris garden, and that was what I did, working all afternoon to prepare the grave, then carrying them out, one by one, in the evening twilight, and laying them out, side by side, face to face in the wet earth. Now it is midnight. Karen Olerud is upstairs, still asleep in her soft prison. I am, to all intents and purposes, alone. Now, at last, I can begin again.

From the moment I first learned to talk, I felt I was being tricked out of something. I remember it still – the memory is clear and indisputable: I am standing in the garden, and Mother is saying the word *rose* over and over, reciting it like a magic spell and pointing to the blossoms on the trellis, sugar-pink and slightly overblown – and I am listening, watching her lips move, still trying to disconnect the flower from the sound. I was already too old to be learning to talk – maybe two, or getting on for three. For a long time, I refused to speak – or so Mother told me. Though I appeared intelligent in other ways, I had problems with language. She had even gone to the doctor about it, but he had told her such things happened, it was quite normal, I would learn to talk sooner or later, in my own time, and I would quickly make up the ground I had lost. He was right. When I did begin speaking, it was a kind of capitulation, as if a tension in my body had broken, and I spoke my first word that afternoon, the word *rose*, meaning that pink, fleshy thing that suddenly flared out from the indescribable continuum of my world, and became an object.

The trick and the beauty of language is that it seems to order the whole universe, misleading us into believing that we live in sight of a rational space, a possible harmony. But if words distance us from the present, so we never quite seize the reality of things, they make an absolute fiction of the past. Now, when I look back, I remember a different world: what must have seemed random and chaotic at the time appears perfectly logical as I tell it, invested with a clarity that even suggests a purpose, a meaning to life. I remember the country around our house as it was before they built the new estates: a dense, infinite darkness filled with sheltering birds and holly trees steeped in the Fifties. I remember the old village: children going from house to house in white sheets, singing and laughing in the dark, waving to us as our car glided by. I remember those months of being alone here, after Mother died. At night, when the land was quiet and still, I would take off my clothes and go naked from room to room, then out into the cool moonlight, wandering amongst the flower beds like an animal, or a changeling from one of Mother's fairy stories. The garden is walled on all sides; no one could see me, and the house was so far from the village that I would hear nothing but the owls in the woods, and the occasional barking of foxes out on the meadow. Sometimes I wondered if I was real – my body would be different, clothed in its own sticky-sweet smell, a smell like sleep, laced with Chanel No. 19 from Mother's dressing table.

When I was a child, Mother would come into the bedroom and tell me stories. It was a ritual she performed, without variation: I had to go up to bed, and she would follow five minutes later. I would hear the clock strike nine as she climbed the stairs. Sometimes she brought a book, but quite often she told me the stories out of her head. Whether she made them up, or had them by heart, I couldn't say, but she never once hesitated or faltered. I had the impression, then, that she knew every story that had ever been told, and all she had to do was think of one for a moment, and every detail came flooding into her mind, instantly. It was Mother who told me the story of Akbar: how he built the Dumb House, not for profit, or even to prove a point, but from pure curiosity. Nobody knows how long it stood, or what happened to the children who were locked inside with their mute attendants. Nobody knows because the story of the Dumb House was only ever an episode in another, much longer story, an anecdote that had been folded in, told in passing to illustrate the personality of Akbar the Mughal, the dyslexic emperor whose collection of manuscripts was the richest in the known world. Later I realised that most of the details of the story were embellishments that Mother had added herself, to spin out this single episode that I liked so much. In fact, the original story of the Dumb House was simple and fleeting. In that version, the Mughal's counsellors were debating whether a child is born with the innate, God-given ability to speak; they had agreed this gift is equivalent in some way to the soul, the one characteristic that marks out the human from the animal.

But Akbar declared that speech is learned, for the very reason that the soul is innate, and the soul does not correspond to any single faculty, whether it be the ability to speak, or to dream, or to reason. Surely, he argued, if speech came from the soul, then there would be only one language, instead of many. But the counsellors disagreed. While it was true that there were many languages, these were simply the corruptions of the original gift, implanted in the soul by God. They knew of incidents in which children had been left in isolation for years, or raised by animals: in such circumstances they had created a language of their own, that nobody else understood, which they could not have learned from others.

Akbar listened. When the counsellors had finished speaking, he told them he would test their hypothesis. He had his craftsmen build a mansion, far from the city: a large, well-appointed house, with its own gardens and fountains. Here Akbar established a court of the mute, into which he introduced a number of new-born babies, gathered from the length and breadth of the Empire. The children were well cared for, and were provided with everything they could possibly need, but because their attendants were dumb, they never heard human speech, and they grew up unable to talk, as Akbar had predicted. People would travel from all over the kingdom to visit the house. They would stand for hours outside its walled gardens, listening to the silence, and for years to come the mansion was known as the Gang Mahal, or Dumb House.

Mother would come to the bedroom and tell me this story in the evenings. Naturally, her version was different; she barely touched upon the controversy over the innateness of language, or the nature of the soul. Instead she described the Gang Mahal in sumptuous detail: the orange trees in terracotta pots, the

10

jewelled walls, the unearthly silence. I lay in bed listening, watching her lips move, intoxicated by her perfume. I used to wonder what had happened when those children grew up; how they thought, if thought was possible, if they ever remembered anything from one moment to the next. There are people who say speech is magical; for them, words have the power to create and destroy. Listening to Mother's stories, I became enmeshed in a view of the world: an expectation, a secret fear. Even now, nothing seems more beautiful to me than language when it creates the impression of order: the naming of things after their true nature; the act of classification; the creation of kingdoms and genera, species and sub-species; the designation of animal, vegetable or mineral, of monocotyledonous plants, freshwater fishes, birds of prey, the periodic table. This is why the past seems perfect, a time of proportion and order, because it is immersed in speech. For animals, memory might reside as a sensation, a resonance in the nerves, or in the meat of the spine. But for humans, the past cannot be described except in words. It is nowhere else. What disturbs me now is the possibility that language might fail: after the experiment ended so inconclusively, I cannot help imagining that the order which seems inherent in things is only a construct, that everything might fall into chaos, somewhere in the long white reaches of forgetting. That is why it is imperative for me to begin again, and that is why Karen was sent here, after all this time, to fulfil her true purpose.

I lived entirely in the presence of my mother. Even when she wasn't there, I was aware of her, somewhere, and I was always conscious of myself, I always behaved as if she were with me, watching and listening. My father, on the other hand, seemed barely present. Most of the time, I disregarded him, just as

Mother did. He seemed peripheral to our existence, irrelevant to our enterprise and, at the time, I thought he preferred it that way. Often, he was away on business. When he was at home, he would make an effort to play the game of father and son, but we were always awkward together. He knew I belonged to Mother.

Not that I was ever disrespectful. When he asked me to take a walk with him, I always assented readily, and we would go out, pretending there was some purpose to our excursion. Usually, he would ask me to go fishing. He had no idea of how fishing was done, but he must have thought it was appropriate, the sort of thing fathers do with their sons. We would carry our rods and baskets to the river, then sit on the bank in silence, watching the water flow over the dark weeds. I was certain the place we usually chose was wholly unsuitable. I never saw a fish there, in all our visits.

We would spend a couple of hours like that, then we would gather up our equipment and turn for home. I think my father enjoyed being near the water. It set him at his ease and, on the way back, he would seem more relaxed; he would make efforts at conversation, asking me questions about school, or what books or music I liked. I would answer as well as I could; I think I wanted to be friendly, but the questions were too simple, too closed. Then, as the conversation petered out, he would fall back on his favourite stand-by, which was to ask if there was anything I wanted, anything I needed. To begin with, I must have thought these questions were nothing more than conversational gambits, and I told him I was fine, there was nothing I could think of. Eventually, when I saw how disappointed he was with this reply, I began naming things, just to keep him happy, and perhaps also to see what would happen. I was surprised to begin with, then later, slightly irritated by the fact that he always remembered what I had asked for. Inevitably, the requested item would arrive: without ceremony, it would appear in the hall, or on the table in the breakfast room. There would be no gift wrap, no tags or ribbons, nothing to say who had sent it. Most often, these gifts were delivered to the house, and usually when my father was away. Mother must have been aware of the parcels, but she made no comment. It was as if they had been delivered to us by accident.

In a spirit of loyalty, I tried to ignore them, too; but I have to admit there were times when I was pleased. My father's interpretation of even my vaguest request would be uncanny. No matter what I asked him for − a bicycle, a new violin, a tennis racquet, a fountain pen − no matter what it was, it would always be the size, the style, the colour I would have chosen. Yet I never felt these objects were gifts as such, because I never felt they were entirely mine. I used them the way I would have used something borrowed, taking care of them the way you might care for something that, sooner or later, would have to be returned. Occasionally I asked for things I didn't really want, to see what he would do. Yet still, no matter what it was, he only chose the best, and I would be embarrassed, as if I had been caught out in a mean practical joke. Sometimes I even forgot what I had asked for. I would just say the first thing that came to mind, to give him something to think about as we made our way home across the meadow. But he always remembered. Whatever I requested would appear, in its plain packaging, like a bundle of exotic flotsam, washed up on the doorstep. Most of the time, he wasn't there for me to thank him. I think he arranged it that way, to avoid any difficulty. Looking back, in spite of his seeming collaboration with our regime, I see that he was secretly and perversely trying to find some way into the world I shared with Mother, and these gifts were his crude attempts to win my confidence. I feel sorry for him now, in retrospect. He must have been lonely; it must have pained him to know he was little more than a stranger to us, someone we treated with courtesy, but whom we regarded, essentially, as a guest in our house.

Nevertheless, I felt guilty sometimes, when the parcels arrived and I stripped them open to find some expensive object that I couldn't use, glittering in the morning light. Occasionally I would go to the river alone and stay there all day, as if paying a forfeit, or enduring some kind of penance. The river seemed different when I was by myself: it was a mysterious place, whose strangeness I was interrupting. Sometimes I took my rod and pretended to fish, for my father's sake. I wanted to tell him I had been out there while he was away, carrying on where we had left off. Sometimes I even convinced myself that I would catch a fish. It would have been good to have something to show him on his return. Most of the time, though, I just took off my shoes and socks and waded out into the cold, quick water, to feel the long streams of riverweed against my shins. My feet would be chilled to the bone, but I still felt the current on my skin, and I would stand for as long as I could, letting the cold sink in, trying to become another element of the river, as natural, as neutral, as the silt and the water. I looked for fish, but I never saw any. I remembered a story Mother had told me once, about an ancient water spirit who lived amongst the weeds in dark ponds and rivers. The spirit was called Jenny Greenteeth, and I suppose, in the book, it was meant to be a woman, but I imagined it as a near-hermaphrodite, part-woman, part-man, part-fish, something wired into the sway of the water, aware of the least flicker or ripple. In my mind, it possessed that special fish-sensitivity where even rainfall is a tapping at the spine; it knew the difference between ordinary disturbances of the surface, and the steps of a child, or the tug of a probing stick. In the book, it was shown as a wrinkled, bone-and-hair fiend, surging from the water, its long nails and jagged teeth coated with weed and moss. But on those visits to the river, I would imagine something subtle, almost invisible. Quick as a pike, it would rise to its prey, then disappear into the depths, but there would be no cries, no blood, no immediate horrors. A deceptive calm would return to the river: birds would sing again, the sun would break through the clouds. The victim would be unaware of what had happened. After a while, he would grow bored, and return home, where no one would notice any change. Yet the change would have happened under the surface, behind the appearance of normality. That child would never be the same again. He would grow into something dark and cold, something that belonged to the river. He would see possibilities that others missed, and he would act upon them. People would begin to see him as a monster, but as far as he was concerned, they were nothing more than phantoms. His world was different from theirs. In his world, their thoughts, their actions, their judgements were immaterial.

In the holidays, when I was home from school, Mother would take me out looking for corpses. To begin with, it was her idea: she wanted me to see how things looked when they were dead, and she got me to come by making a game of it, an odd form of hide and seek. She said every animal had a place of its own where it would go to die if it could; wild animals wanted to be alone when they were sick or dying, and they would crawl away into the undergrowth, to be out of the light and the wind. The only dead things I had seen until then were pheasants and hedgehogs on the road to the village, but Mother had a gift for knowing where to look: animals I had only ever encountered in books became real as corpses, life-size, as it were, with hard claws and tiny, blood-threaded teeth, flesh I could prod and turn, fur I could stroke, disturbing the flies, drawing the cold or the warmth of decay through the palm of my hand. As we searched for fresh bodies, we would revisit the sites of earlier finds. There was always something new to see, something strangely beautiful – not only in summer, when the bodies imploded slowly and the smell was dark and sickly, but also in autumn and winter, when they lay for weeks, cold and untarnished, frozen voles laid out on the grass, small birds lying under the hedges with their legs stretched, their eyes clenched and wrinkled. It was odd, but as I followed the process of decay, there seemed to be something curative in it all, as if the animal was being renewed, or purified, leaching away in the rain, drying in the sun, vanishing slowly, leaving behind only a faint yellowish aftermath in the grass, in which form was implicit, with a half-life of its own.

After a while, I started going out on these hunts alone. At some level, at the level of an undercurrent, I had begun to think it might be possible to be incorporated into this process in some way; or rather, I began to form a primitive, superstitious notion that I could make it work for my own purposes, propitiating it with small offerings, vague gestures of rehearsal and assent. At school we performed an experiment with moulds, sealing a piece of moistened bread in a jar and leaving it in a warm place to see the lime-green and ochre life-forms growing on the surface, and I repeated this experiment at home, unscrewing the lid of the jar each day for the sweet perfume of new life arising from decay, probing the black and silvery hairs, watching them blossom and collapse in their hundreds. I varied the contents of the jar: lemon rind, scraps of meat, cabbage leaves, egg-yolk – everything had its own way of becoming something new, and I made my own private catalogue of implosions and seepages, ergots and mildews, sickening odours, twitches, vanishings. One afternoon I loosened a tangle of hair from Mother's brush, wrapped it in tissue paper and buried it out in the garden amongst her irises, so the freshening rain could wear it down and make it new, irresistibly, in the cold earth. That same year I began to collect the skulls and bones of the animals I found, laying them out on beds of sawdust in old shoe boxes, giving each its own label to show the date and place where it had been found. I think even then I knew what I was doing, but at the same time it had the quality of a game – as if I were preventing myself from fully understanding that these rituals, these clumsy flirtations with death and renewal, were really my childish attempts to prevent Mother from dying. I remember that there was an afternoon, around that time, when it first came home to me that she was mortal. Of course, I must have known before then that she would die, but there had never been real understanding, the idea of her death had always been vague, lacking in intimacy.

I think there are places in the mind where nothing changes: a garden shed, the space beneath a bridge, the urine-scented steps to an old air-raid shelter littered with rags and broken glass. It may be that what happened in those places are the moments you would choose to remember clearly if you could, the scenes you erase without knowing you have erased them, the events that populate your dreams in muted form, which you abandon in waking, a deliberate yet poignant loss. If only you could remember, something would be whole again; even if the memory was difficult to accept, it would be better than the not-knowing which has defined and limited you for years, making you weak and irresolute, a creature attuned to fear, incapable of fully assenting to your own life. This is a psychologist's cliché, and yet I accept it, almost unconditionally. I have no clear idea of what happened to me, one summer's day, out hunting in the grass. I picture a man in a grubby business suit, strangely out of place amongst the cow parsley and wild geraniums. I picture him taking hold of me, pressing me to a fence, and fumbling at my groin – but this is all there is for sure, an imagined act, no more convincing or immediate than a scene from a book or a film. I have one clear memory of an overwhelming powerlessness, of being unable to move, or struggle free. As far as I recall, he did not speak: whatever it was that happened, took place in silence. Then I remember running home across the meadow – and this memory is perfectly clear – I remember finding the door to our walled garden locked and thinking it was part of a conspiracy, thinking someone inside the walls was in league with the man who had caught me out there. I shouted and hammered desperately at the locked door until Mother came and opened it. She stood looking at me quizzically, with her secateurs in her hand, slightly mocking, as if she wanted me to understand, of my own accord, that I was making a fuss about nothing.

'What is it?' she said, after a moment. 'You're all dirty.'

'The gate was locked.'

'Well, there's no need to get upset. You only had to knock.'

'I was locked out,' I repeated. I could hear how loud my voice was, how unacceptably vehement.

She shook her head.

'Go and get cleaned up,' she said. 'You look like something the cat dragged in.'

She didn't seriously enquire as to what had happened and I think, even then, I was already beginning to erase what it was from my mind, forgetting for her sake, as much as my own. She looked so clean, so untouchable, yet at the heart of that perfection there was something soft, something she preserved by an effort, as the shellfish preserves its soft white body, by continually renewing its shell. It was then that I first understood how vulnerable she was, and I felt sorry for her, as if I had caught her out, not so much in a lie as in a pitiful act of self-deception.

For months afterwards I was afraid she would become ill and die. I watched her carefully for symptoms: if she fell asleep in the evening, sitting in her chair, a book or a garden magazine sliding to the floor as she drifted away, I woke her immediately. At night I would stand outside her bedroom, to hear if she was still breathing. In the daytime, when I was at school, I carried a pair of her gloves in my coat pocket, taking them out from time to time to make sure I still had them. It was one of those games children play to cheat fate – if I lost the gloves, Mother would die, but as long as I kept them, she would be invulnerable. In addition to these rituals of deceit and propitiation, I gave myself the task of listing by name all the flowers in her garden: first the irises, which she prized more than the others, then the lilies, the pinks, the roses, the shrubs and climbers, the fruit trees trained against the walls. When that was finished I moved on to something else, compiling lists of scientific terms and place names in special notebooks that I kept hidden under my bed, alongside the shoe boxes full of animal skulls.

Perhaps my anxiety was justified. For some reason, that was a year of surprising and unexplained deaths. During the spring term alone, three children in my school were buried. It was strange to know people who were dead: I remember feeling their ghosts around me, buttoned-up and freshly combed, ghosts of the daylight, coming home from school in raincoats and fur-lined boots, mysterious for having failed to live that far: Alana Fuller, who died in her bed one night, tucked-up and quiet; Stuart Gow, run over in the street in front of the whole school at home-time; a Polish boy whose name I forget, who died from the injuries inflicted by his father one night in a drunken rage. Then there were the strangers: the men who died in a mining accident; the little unidentified boy who was found strangled and half-naked in a ditch on the road to Weston. The one that fascinated me most was the death of a woman who lived on the other side of the village. When they broke into her house, they found her decaying under a veil of blowflies. She had been there for days, as still as her strange keepsakes: the box of hair in the tallboy, the Indian miniatures, the bedside drawer full of confetti and flakes of paper snow. I remember thinking how wonderful it would have been, to walk into that room and find her there, with her whole life gathered around her.

But Mother did not die, not that year. Some time in the autumn, though, she became ill. The doctor was called, and I started making my lists in Latin rather than English, because Latin gave me a sense of time as intimate and continuous, all history only a moment away, something I could see from my own house: a movement in the fields beyond our garden walls, a soft, deep sound, like damsons falling in the dark, falling continually and melting into the wet grass. There was nothing mystical about the world as I experienced it; there was no supernatural, but there was something mysterious there, a force that could be recognised, and with which I felt I could negotiate. That was how Latin operated. It dispelled the idea of the supernatural, but it retained the sense of the mysterious; it defined and classified, but it did not limit. Perhaps the strategy worked: though she was ill for several weeks, Mother recovered, and life went on as before.

Later, when she did die, I found myself repeating those rituals, to no real end, other than to resurrect the past. In the evenings, when it was cool, I would go out alone, poking among the nettles and balsam along the riverbank, crossing the meadow where the owls hunt, but I had less success than I had when Mother was with me. Most of the time, I just went out for the sensation of being in the open, touched by the wind, feeling my body cool after the day's warmth. On other days I would drive out to the graveyard and look at Mother's headstone. When she first died, I still felt that she was close: the house contained her perfume and the other scents and textures I associated with her, honey, steamed fruits, various powders. Even as I added to this web of smell and colour, I was still the keeper of her ghost; nothing I did replaced any part of that phantom's complex presence. It was as if she was still there, on the air. But later she grew remote and I began to feel it was the stone that had caused the change – as if by setting in place this permanent marker to her life I was actually erasing it forever, letting her slip away to the dry, limitless space of the fairy stories she used to tell.

I have no clear memory of the moment when the idea for the experiment came to me. It was written into my mind from the start, as much a part of me as the love I bore for Mother, as much a piece of my soul as her scent or the sound of her voice, reaching back through my existence to a point before memory, to the very origin of being. If I had to explain it, I would say this: I knew what I wanted to do, and I knew what I was expected to do – by other people, by myself, it didn't matter. Every time I found myself making decisions, it was because I had to reconcile the two – the desire and the expectation – and the desire always won. It's laughable, looking back, to see the processes I went through, pretending to make a reasoned decision. No choice is ever made on the basis of logic; the logic is fabricated around the impulse, the initial desire which is innate and incontrovertible. All the time, I knew where I was going, the elements of my fulfilment or ruin were always present; I only had to work my way into that seam of desire and find the hidden vein of dross or gold. It's not a question of predestination, it's just that free will and destiny are illusions, false opposites, consolations. In the end, they are one and the same: a single process. You choose what you choose and it could not have been otherwise: the choice is destiny. It was there all along, but any alternative you might have considered is an absurd diversion, because it is in your nature to make one choice rather than another. That is identity. To speak of freedom or destiny is absurd because it suggests there is something outside yourself, directing your life, where really it is of the essence: identity, the craftwork of the soul.

So it seems as if I remember one afternoon, not long after Mother died, I was driving home from Wales, when the thought came to me – how do we know the experiment would have ended as it did, in the silence of those children? There was no scientific account, and all the other stories of such ventures were badly documented or unreliable. For a while after Mother died, I was addicted to travel. I would make long journeys for no reason, usually stopping overnight in some village off the main route, some place I had never visited, that had no significance other than its position, or its name – Peas Pottage, Ready Token, Woodmancote. I would see a road sign, or glimpse a steeple in the distance, and I would turn off at the next junction. The villages were usually quiet when I arrived. Sometimes a girl would be sitting on a bench outside the post office, like a memorised image from a daydream, dark-haired, slender, faintly ethereal in her school blouse and pleated skirt. Or a boy would be playing football under a streetlamp. No matter how remote the place, no matter how unlike my own village, there was always an element of homecoming in these arrivals, finding the church or the green in the gold light of the late afternoon, entering a child's landscape and finding its landmarks as if I had studied the maps for years. Often these strange villages seemed more familiar than my own. Sometimes I would stop in the square; sometimes I drove on till the road narrowed and disappeared into a barley field or a stand of alders. I would sleep in the car, if I could, then drive on the next morning.

There was no purpose in any of this. By moving from one place to the next, never speaking more than a few words to anyone, choosing my stops at random, eating and sleeping only when necessary, I managed to create an illusion of floating, of being detached from the human world – a casual visitor, not necessarily of the same species. I could say that this was the illusion I needed at the time, and I understand people who think that way, working things through, considering their motives and needs and making informed decisions. But it all seems too deliberate, put like that. I would rather imagine some force guiding me on a specific and inevitable course towards the Dumb House. I am not even sure if this force should be seen as external, or even if the question is relevant. All I know is that, during those weeks when I was on the road, I was changing. I was becoming capable of carrying out my plans, however vague they were at the time. Happiness, or fulfilment, or whatever else you choose to call it, seems to me to consist of a glimpse of the world as a patterned and limited whole. Or to put it more simply, order comes from without; it is not imposed, not forced. All I wanted was to accommodate that guiding energy, to let its undercurrent work, as if it were a shadow in my body, at a physical, nerve and bone level.

Things rarely happen by chance. That afternoon, on my drive home, I stopped at Silbury Hill to look at a new crop circle that had appeared in a field, directly to the south of the mound. It was a clear day; the path to the hill was narrow, overgrown in places with tall grasses and wild geraniums. I walked around the base, looking for a gap in the fence where I could get through. Then, slowly, I climbed into a new region of wind and light. It was amazing how different it was up there: swifts wheeled and turned overhead; even before I had reached the halfway point, the world below had dwindled and flattened, like the country on a map – cattle and jackdaws wandering in the grass, the cars on the road small and distant. People were sitting in twos and threes on the summit, smoking and drinking orange juice or beer. Most were New-Age travellers, but some were ordinary passers-by, who had stopped on their way to somewhere else, intrigued by the possibility of a new intelligence. One man had driven that morning from Port Talbot. He started telling me his hypothesis about the circles, a mixture of chaos theory and arcane beliefs. The figure itself was intricate and mysterious – not a circle at all, but an elaborate design, like the pattern in old Celtic jewellery or rock carvings. At the head was a large, perfect ring, surmounted by a crescent shape, like the horns of a bull, or a pagan god; to the west, this form was joined by a fine straight line to another structure, composed of four identical circles in a round, and completed by a long, incurving tail. The travellers were calling it The Scorpion.

I was at ease there. I understood what those people wanted; they were tired of the world they had been obliged to accept, a world of facts and limits. They wanted something that was open to interpretation. Each one probably had his or her explanation of the circles, like the man from Port Talbot, but there were no certainties, there was always a space for mystery. That was probably the explanation for the fanciful or incomplete nature of their theories – it was a game they were playing, and part of the game was to avoid the factual, to flirt at the edges of the absurd.

While I was there, I felt there was nothing to stop me from getting into the car and driving away, back towards the west, moving from one crop disturbance to the next, pretending I was solving the mystery, growing into it, vanishing from the world I had inhabited all my life. I could have become someone else as easily as that; maybe I could even have become the person I had suspected all along, less clearly defined, but also less contained. I could make a game of my own life, like those people I had read about in magazines – the woman who disappears on her way home from work; the man who steps out one summer morning to buy a newspaper, or a loaf of bread, and never returns. He is an ordinary man, quite sane, no known problems – or nothing serious at least. He cannot have gone far, dressed as he is in a shirt and a pair of jeans; he only has five pounds in his pocket, but nobody ever sees him again.

That was when the idea of the experiment began to form in my mind. For the first time, I understood the possibility of making something abstract into a real event. I had no clear plan, but the sense of freedom was unexpectedly powerful. It was like a religious conversion: suddenly the hypothesis, the shadow, the distant image, had become a presence, as tangible as flesh and bone. It would have been easy to mistake this sensation for a thing of the moment, a sudden and spontaneous decision, but the idea of the Dumb House experiment had been waiting to form all my life. Even when I first heard that story, I recognised its importance. Maybe at first it was just the image that attracted me: a house in the desert – a palace really – silent, luxurious, filled with crazed or ecstatic children, locked into a world that was permanently mysterious, a whole world of things that they could not describe or define. When God made Adam, he told him to go into the garden and give names to the trees and the animals, and when Adam returned, God saw that these names were good. Presumably the names had not existed before Adam created them. So the children of the Dumb House knew the world as God did: their Eden was always newly-created, as it was in the beginning.

On the other hand, what if the names Adam had chosen were exactly those that God had used, when he summoned the rocks and trees and creatures of the world from nothingness? If that were so, these names would be the nouns of an original language, something that was lost after the Fall, and if those nouns could be rediscovered, they would give a new meaning to the world. Everything, then, would be inviolate, and inviolable. Peace would return to the earth. There had been people who believed this in every age, just as Akbar had believed that language was learned. There was a story about James IV of Scotland, who kept a child in a lonely hut, away from the court; according to Herodotus, the Pharaoh, Psamtik I, had conducted a similar experiment, deciding that the children he had deprived of language were capable of speaking the original tongue, the innate speech upon which Akbar's counsellors had founded their faith.

As far as I was concerned, these stories were misleading and childish. But the story of Akbar and the Dumb House held my attention; I formed images, not only of the house itself, but of those who had initiated the experiment, those who had to live with its consequences. The story does not tell us what happened to the children, and we know nothing of how the counsellors responded when they heard that their faith in the innateness of speech had been undermined, but I could picture a tidy and ordered world crumbling around them. It is easy to understand why they wanted language to be indicative of something divine, an essential and transcendent soul. They had only to look around at the sheer number of people in the world to know that grace, or art, or power – any of the achievements of any one individual – would be insignificant, in the context of that mass of humanity, unless there was something more to reckon with. For religious reasons, their tendency would be to link the soul with the intellect, and the single most significant indicator of intellect is the ability to speak. They might even have believed that thought and language were interdependent, that a being without language would be incapable of thinking. Akbar's answer to the question, and his proposed method of proof, must have struck them as an unimaginable horror – they must have been confident that the Mughal would be proven wrong. So later, when the children were found to be incapable of speech, the counsellors must have considered themselves responsible, in some part, for an appalling act of torture, as they witnessed the infants, empty-minded and soulless, wandering helplessly in an unnamed world. They must have asked themselves what kind of world that was – how terrible, how beautiful, how frightening in its autonomy, in its refusal to be defined. In the end, they must even have regretted the experiment for their own sakes. For surely their faith must have foundered on the outcome. Perhaps it would have decayed slowly, over months, or even years of lingering doubt, but eventually it must have died. It would have been a personal tragedy for each of those men to be parties to an act whose consequences they did not understand.

Yet what they accepted as the final outcome was not a conclusion at all, but a new beginning. That was what Mother had made me see. She had shown me the horror of the children's predicament, through the counsellors' eyes; at the same time, she had let me understand the beauty of the experiment, through the image of the Dumb House itself: perfect, inscrutable, shining in my mind, like a proposition in geometry, or one of those logical paradoxes that, by itself, can open up a whole new field of thought.

For the first few days after I stopped travelling, I worked in the garden and thought about what I wanted to do. I had left the iris beds and rose borders to fend for themselves ever since Mother's death, and the whole place was untidy and overgrown. Now, as I worked, the plants reappeared, complete with their names – and with them emerged my basic plan. I would begin by collecting all the information I could about language learning and deprivation. I would research speech disorders, elective mutism, the wild boys and wolf children of legend, the creators of secret languages and scripts. I would add to the body of research myself, perhaps, trawling through specialist publications and the general press for case histories, anecdotes, hearsay – anything that would help me find what I was looking for – and I would place an advertisement in the local paper asking for personal, previously undocumented experiences. I would leave the wording deliberately vague, to encourage a wide response.

Naturally, though, I still felt something was missing. I knew that the only way to test the hypothesis was to repeat the experiment and, from the beginning, that was my true intention. Nevertheless, I telephoned the *County Herald* and placed an advertisement. I deliberated for some time on where it should be printed, but in the end there was no alternative but to put it in the personal columns, among the Tarot readings and lonely hearts, the exclusive massages and the appeals for information about people half-met in palm houses and tea rooms. There was something about the Personals – something in the language used – that suggested autumn: I had probably read too many books where the lovers come splashing through fallen leaves in scarves and winter coats. It is always Sunday afternoon, there is always a lamp burning in the middle distance, probably even a smell of toast and warm butter, or the sound of a violin being played in some rented room in the backstreets. I liked the idea of my clinical, tersely-worded piece appearing there, as a form of rebuke, a cold, sharp instrument amongst the love hearts and the bad poems.

Meanwhile, I began visiting the reference library in Weston, to collect what information I could not find in books from Mother's study. The historical evidence was apocryphal. The earliest language experiment I could find was that recorded by Herodotus: in his second history he describes how Psamtik gave two new born babies to a shepherd, to keep hidden among his flocks. He told the man that no one should utter a word in the presence of these children, but they should live by themselves, in a lonely place. It was the shepherd's task to keep them fed, and 'perform the other things needful'. Psamtik commanded these things, said Herodotus, because he desired, when the babes should be past meaningless whimpering, to hear what language they would utter first. One day, after two years had passed, when the shepherd went into the children's house, they fell down before him and cried *becos*, and stretched out their hands. The shepherd brought the king to see the children, and they repeated the word *becos* which, in Phrygian, means bread. Herodotus concludes his account by saying that the Pharaoh was forced to accept that the Phrygians were the oldest race on earth, and not the Egyptians, as he had previously maintained.

It was an amusing story, but it was pure fairy tale. Other accounts were similar, for example that of James IV's Hebrew-speaking child. In some cases, the children did not speak, or they simply died from loneliness and neglect, as in the experiment conducted by Frederick II of Hohenstaufen. None of these accounts had the simple beauty of the Akbar story, but it was interesting that the theme had fascinated historians throughout the ages. There were cases of wolf-boys, calf-children, infants raised by gazelles, pigs, bears and leopards. The stories came from as far afield as Japan and Germany, India and Ohio. The two best-documented contemporary accounts – the cases of Genie and the Kennedy twins – were utterly contradictory. Genie had been kept isolated in a small room by her parents, who thought she was retarded. Her father had built her a chair, a little like a commode, which allowed her to be kept confined all day, without doing herself harm. At night she was strapped to a bed. She existed like this for the first thirteen years of her life. As far as anyone could tell, she had never been exposed to language and, most of the time, she had been alone.

When Genie was discovered, the linguists and grammarians were very excited. The accepted wisdom – the Lenneberg hypothesis – stated that a child deprived of language between the age of two and puberty would never learn to speak grammatically. They might learn individual words, but they would not be able to string them together to form meaningful sentences. Considerable resources were expended in teaching Genie first, sign language, then speech, but she never progressed to sentence formation, and, for legal, rather than scientific reasons, the experiment ended in confusion, with Genie confined to an institution.

As far as I could tell, the problem with the Genie experiment had been as much a lack of history as a lack of control. From the first, the researchers must have known that they could never collect enough useful data on Genie's early life to support a hypothesis: the very name they chose for her gave them away, for what was Genie but a creature who emerged, fully-formed, from the darkness? She had been sealed in a bottle for years, but nobody knew what had happened inside the bottle; nobody knew if she was subnormal, as her father had claimed, or even how far she had been exposed to language. In her thirteen years, she must have heard something. Nobody could say why she had never developed speech: they assumed that, because she had been kept in isolation, she'd had no opportunity to do so. Yet, when Grace and Virginia Kennedy were found, after being confined for several years (for the same reason as Genie, because their parents had considered them retarded), they had created their own, relatively sophisticated language, even inventing names for one another. They called themselves Poto and Cabenga. Was it because they had each other; was it the case that what mattered wasn't so much exposure to language as the possibility of a listener? Did Genie fail to talk because she'd heard almost no speech in her formative years? Or was it because she had nobody to talk to?

The few examples I found of Poto and Cabenga's speech fascinated me. The language they had invented was strangely beautiful, and I studied it carefully, convinced it was authentic. However, the books in the library contained only fleeting and tantalising references to these histories. In each case, the children themselves disappeared into a kind of limbo, where I could not follow. The Kennedy girls were probably in their early thirties, if they were still alive. Genie was discovered in 1970, at the age of thirteen. What happened to them? And how many more children might there be, hidden away in damp rooms, shackled to their beds, or strapped into homemade commodes?

For the first week after I placed the advertisement, I heard nothing. Then, when replies did start coming through, they were mostly irrelevant, or sarcastic, sometimes even obscene. But there was one that looked promising. I remember the letter clearly, the pale-blue paper, the deliberate, overly ornate script. It came from a woman who lived nearby with her seven-year-old son. The boy was mute, she said, but there was no physiological cause; the woman had been to doctors, speech therapists, psychologists – she told me all this in that first letter – but it had made no difference. To begin with, I was suspicious. There was something in the tone of her letter that suggested she imagined I was offering a cure of some kind; a solution, or at least an explanation. But after a while I understood that all she wanted was to tell somebody else her story, someone who had never heard it before. She gave an address, but no telephone number; she lived in Weston, just twelve miles away. She suggested I call on her, on any weekday evening, between five and eight thirty. Her name was Mrs Olerud; her son's name was Jeremy.

I tried to picture the woman from her letter. I supposed the name was Scandinavian; certainly, there was something about the way she wrote – an openness, combined with an odd formality – that suggested a foreigner. I read the letter several times; it ran for several pages, and was mostly a history of the boy's life, his illnesses, his school grades, the minor accidents he had suffered. Each doctor he had seen was mentioned by name, as if she expected me to be familiar with his specialism and methods. There was no mention of the boy's father; it occurred to me that the man might disapprove of her opening up to a complete stranger like this, or perhaps he was simply unaware that she had written to me. Whenever she talked about the boy, I had a distinct impression of distaste or unease. It was if she was afraid of her own child; or of someone else whose view of the child differed from hers, someone who was looking over her shoulder all the time. There was too much respect. Yes, that was it. She never used pronouns in her descriptions of the boy; she always referred to him by name. There was a kind of awe that overwhelmed her whenever she mentioned her son. I think it was this, as much as anything else, that roused my curiosity. I wanted to see this child. I wanted to see him because the letter had suggested to me that his mother was afraid of him, and I wanted to know why a grown woman would be afraid of a seven-year-old.

Twenty-six, Hartskill Road was one of a set of pebble-dashed former council houses at the end of a short terrace. I was surprised when I eventually found it; I had expected a much better neighbourhood. The other houses were grey-brown, but Mrs Olerud's was painted white, so it looked like a piece of wedding cake left out to crumble and dry in the evening sunlight. None of the gardens was well-tended, but number twenty-six was particularly untidy, overgrown with bindweed and huge patches of Yorkshire Fog, it looked like a patch of waste ground. There was even a bed of nettles against a fence; the only sign that this piece of land had once been a garden was the odd clump of pinks, or a mildewed rose, struggling to exist amongst the weeds. The front door was blistered and cracked, as if someone had been stripping the paint and had given up half way through the job, leaving a sticky white skin of undercoat to the hazards of sunlight and frost. The window frames were intact, but the blue paintwork was scabbed and broken in places; one of the windows was cracked, and the doorbell did not ring. I knocked; waited.

The woman who opened the door was quite out of place in this house. She was wearing a fine-quality print dress and white, high-heeled shoes; she looked as if she had just come home from a wedding, or a garden party. She was wearing make-up, and I caught a hint of a good, not inexpensive perfume. Ten years before, she would have been considered pretty; now, with the lines around her mouth and the stain of persistent disappointment in her eyes, she was almost beautiful. Her eyes were bright blue, with the pure mineral colour of precious stones.

'Mrs Olerud?'

'Yes.' Her manner was formal, a little remote, as if she suspected she should remember me from somewhere.

'You said I might call.' I said. 'In your letter?'

Her face remained blank.

'I would have telephoned before I came,' I continued, 'but I don't have a number for you.'

'I haven't got a telephone,' she said. 'Is this about Jeremy?'

'Yes.'

Her expression altered. There was still no sign that she understood who I was, but the fact that I was calling about the boy had obviously broken through her defences.

'You'd better come in,' she said.

Inside, the house was tastefully decorated, if a little sparsely furnished. The sitting room contained two armchairs, a low coffee table, a high bookcase with open shelves covered in photographs in plain silver frames. It was evident that the woman had a modicum of taste, and that she preferred to buy nothing at all if she could not afford something decent. She offered me a chair and I sat down, next to the fireplace. On the wall above the mantelpiece what looked like an original water colour of a woodland landscape was hanging in a simple, black and silver frame. It was well-executed, though a little too pretty for my taste. I knew immediately, from the expression on her face, that the woman had painted it herself.

She sat down in the chair opposite and looked at me closely. She was totally lacking in self-consciousness: she studied my face, my clothes, my hands, as if she was trying to read my character, or my intentions, from my physical appearance. She stared at me for a minute, perhaps longer. I sat still, returning her look, trying to seem unperturbed. It occurred to me, now I was in her house, that I had no idea of how to proceed. She probably expected questions, perhaps something official – a form, or a questionnaire. Without the necessary qualifications, how would I explain my interest without seeming morbid, or a little mad? I waited for her to speak. If she asked questions, I would make something up – a study, a doctoral thesis.

'Would you like some tea?' she said, at last.

'That would be nice,' I answered.

'Please make yourself at home,' she said. 'I won't be long.'

I felt uneasy. I was excited by the unexpected appearance of this beautiful woman, in such unlikely surroundings, but I wasn't altogether sure what to make of her. There was something unsettling about her. On the one hand, she was formal, even exaggeratedly polite in her speech, yet the way she looked at me, the way she moved made it seem that I did not really exist in her eyes, or at least, that I did not exist enough for her to feel she should adapt her behaviour to my presence. By now, I was certain she lived alone with her silent child. There was no Mr Olerud – perhaps there never had been – and after years of solitude, she had forgotten how to act in the presence of other adults. She knew the words and the gestures, but the meaning had disappeared.

I walked over to the bookcase, with its rows of photographs in silver frames. Mostly they showed Mrs Olerud, either alone, or with an elderly couple I took to be her parents. The older photographs – those taken around ten or twelve years before – showed a much brighter, more attractive version of the woman I had just met. The eyes were just as blue, just as penetrating, but there was a look of amused expectation that made the young woman in the photograph appear exquisitely desirable. I noticed there were no pictures of children.

Mrs Olerud returned, with a tray of tea things: a bone china teapot, some cups and saucers, and a small, rose-patterned plate of shortbread fingers.

'I hope you like lemon,' she said. 'I haven't got any milk.'

'Lemon is fine,' I answered, smiling.

She did not return the smile. She put the tray on the coffee table and began to pour. The tea was transparent, almost colourless.

'I'm afraid it's not very strong,' she said.

'That's fine for me,' I replied, still smiling. This time she smiled back faintly, as if to apologise for the weakness of the tea.

There was an awkward silence. It was as if she was waiting for me to speak, to explain myself, and I realised I had nothing to say. I had made no preparation for our meeting; I had no idea what I would do when I met the child. I had no props, no credentials; in all likelihood, she would take me for an impostor, or worse. I tried to think of something to say, something technical, something scientific. My mind was blank. Finally, to break the silence, Mrs Olerud began asking me questions: how far I had come, what work I did, whether I had any children of my own. The manner in which she presented the questions suggested a system, as if she had read a guide on how to make small talk; I might have imagined she was interviewing me, except that she hardly appeared to register my answers to her questions and I was sure, if I had asked her to repeat what I had said, ten or twenty minutes later, she would have forgotten everything. She seemed apprehensive; I had the impression that she was nervous about letting me see the boy. The talk was a diversion, nothing more. She asked no questions about my intentions or my method of working. She asked for no identification, or credentials. She didn't even mention the child. I was beginning to think she had forgotten why I had come, or perhaps that she had changed her mind, and would send me away without seeing her son, when she stopped talking and looked at me sadly, the resignation in her face quite undisguised.

'I imagine you'd like to see Jeremy now,' she said.

'If it's convenient.'

'Of course. I'll fetch him. I keep him upstairs in the evenings.'

She smiled – that same faint, apologetic smile – and went out to fetch the boy. I wondered what she meant by keeping him upstairs. Was he confined in some way? Bedridden? Bound? I listened, but I heard nothing out of the ordinary: footsteps on the landing, a moment's pause, then more footsteps, descending the stairs. I drank some tea, and tried to look neutral, like a casual visitor, when the boy entered the room – though it occurred to me that casual visitors were probably scarce in that house, and for a moment I had a fleeting thought that neither the child nor the woman had seen anyone in months, even years. But that was absurd; if he was seven years old, he would go to school. His grandparents would visit. He would have doctor's appointments, trips to the dentist, a normal life, like any seven-year-old.

As soon as I saw him, I understood why Mrs Olerud was afraid. He was thin and pale, small for his age, with wild, yellowish hair, like Struwelpeter in the old children's story. His eyes were as blue as his mother's, but they were hard and opaque, like metal. He walked quickly into the room and stood looking at me in surprise. I was struck by the overwhelming sense of something animal in his presence, an unbelievable tension; he was like a black hole, an intensity that drew energy from everyone around him, and gave back nothing.

I glanced at Mrs Olerud. Once again, I had an image of the child in a cage, or locked into the midden of his room, squatting on the floor, crunching on bones like the feral children in legends. Yet he was reasonably clean and, except for his hair, he looked presentable. He was wearing a pair of dungarees over a red and blue striped shirt. They were good enough clothes; his mother had probably chosen them carefully, to set off his light colouring. Nevertheless, I felt uncomfortable. There was something in the boy's manner that suggested an almost unbearable dread, a sense of horrified anticipation.

They stood in the doorway for some time. Mrs Olerud said nothing. I felt she was simply showing me the boy; he could have been a leopard or a wild dog, some dangerous creature that had somehow come to live in her house, and she was letting me see it, so I would know what she had to endure. I wanted to say something, to break the tension, but I could not bring myself to speak directly to the child.

'Can he hear me, if I talk to him?' I asked.

'I don't know,' she replied. 'Sometimes he seems to understand, but he never does anything to show it. He doesn't – respond.'

The way she spoke the last word underlined how inappropriate it seemed to be talking like this in front of her son. Then she shrugged almost imperceptibly.

'I thought you would like to see him,' she said. 'But he ought to go back now. It's easier if he stays upstairs in the evenings.'

She touched the boy's shoulder and they left the room without a word. The child did not look back. I heard them climbing the stairs, crossing the landing. I wanted to call them back, to see more of the boy, but I was too surprised to speak.

When Mrs Olerud returned, she seemed relieved. She sounded brighter; I thought she was making light of things.

'Your tea must be getting cold,' she said. She was matter of fact, but she could not altogether hide the effort.

'What did you mean?' I asked. 'When you said it was easier if he stayed in his room – what did you mean exactly?'

She looked uncomfortable, as if I had caught her out in a deception.

'He gets restless,' she said. 'He doesn't sleep well at the best of times. Any excitement in the evening only makes it worse.'

'But you told me to come in the evening. You ought to have suggested another time, if this was inconvenient.'

She looked puzzled for a moment, as if she was surprised at what I had said.

'I'm sorry,' she said. 'Today has been difficult. Perhaps you could come again, another time.'

'Does he go to school?'

She did not answer.

'He must have special needs,' I persisted.

'Yes.'

'Which school does he go to?'

She looked at me sharply.

'I have to be getting on,' she said quickly, in a near singsong. 'I have to get him ready for bed. Would it be convenient for you to call again some time?'

She stood up, to make it clear that she wanted me to leave. Evidently the questions had annoyed her, and it occurred to me again that she had something to hide. I had no choice but to comply with her wishes, but I was in half a mind, as I left, to give up on this case before it even started. The boy was probably retarded, or emotionally disturbed. The causes of his speech problem were almost certainly buried in the past, and I doubted Mrs Olerud's willingness to help uncover them.

I think she sensed this; as she was showing me out, she stopped and laid her hand on my arm. I was struck again by the shadow of the beauty in her face.

'Do come back,' she said. 'I'm sorry about tonight. It's just that today has been difficult.'

I nodded.

'You will come again?'

We were standing in the hallway, at the foot of the stairs. It occurred to me that the boy could hear us, if he was listening, and I wondered if he understood. All of a sudden I realised why Mrs Olerud had responded to my advertisement. She had no expectation that I would be able to help her son, and no real interest in my studies. She had written to me because she was lonely, and too proud to go out looking for help or companionship of her own volition. This way, I had come to her, and now she was afraid of losing that contact.

'I'm not sure,' I answered. I was still annoyed. 'I'm not sure I know why you wanted me to come. It's not as if I can help. I'm just doing research – do you see?'

'Yes,' she said. 'I do, truly.' Her voice was too high, too sincere.

'I can't help you,' I repeated.

'I don't want help. I want to help you if I can. With your – studies.'

She hesitated, watching me. Her hand was still clutching my arm. I could see she was trying to think of something else to say, to put me at my ease, so I would come again.

'Come on Saturday,' she said. 'In the daytime. It's easier in the daytime.'

She was animated now, almost desperate. When I had arrived, she had seemed not to know who I was, or why I had come. She had been distant, almost indifferent. Nothing had passed between us, except small talk; she had shown me the boy, then told me to leave, more or less unceremoniously. Now she was pleading with me to return. I might have been angry with her: her behaviour had been rude, and unnecessarily mysterious. Instead, I was intrigued. Karen Olerud possessed a quality that I recognised, even at that first meeting.

'Saturday,' she said again.

'Perhaps,' I answered. 'If I can. When would be convenient?'

'Two o'clock?'

'Fine.' I wanted to sound noncommittal, as if I still hadn't decided whether to keep the appointment.

'I'll expect you at two then,' she said, and as she opened the door, her expression became neutral again. It was as if, with her anxiety, something else was bleeding away, and the last picture I had of her was the image of an empty, impassive face, a contrived and practised absence, a kind of nothingness.

I returned the next morning. At seven thirty I parked the car at the end of the street, so I had a clear view of the house, and waited. I wanted to see Jeremy leave for school and what Mrs Olerud did when she was alone. I did not trust what she had told me in the letter – I had no evidence, other than her word, that the child really was dumb. He might be disturbed, but it was just as likely that his mother was the one with the problem. The boy might have chosen his silence, or he might have had silence forced upon him. I told myself that that was my motive for being there; yet, at the same time, I have to confess that I was less interested in the boy than in his mother. Something had passed between us the previous evening. I had lain awake half the night, thinking about her, remembering her face, and the feel of her hand on my arm. I think, from the first,

I guessed what was about to happen. I had brought her flowers from the garden; even though it seemed quite inappropriate, I felt sure she would accept them.

It was a damp morning. It had rained in the night and the gardens were still wet. As soon as the sun came up, everything began to steam; clouds of vapour unfurled from the larchlap fences, a fine mist formed on the hedges and lawns. Soon it was warm. The light streamed through the gaps between the houses, catching on car mirrors and headlamps, investing the run-down estate with a ghostly and transient beauty. There was no sign of Mrs Olerud or her son. Other children appeared on the street, girls in blue dresses, boys in uniform. One or two saw me and peered into the car, but mostly they passed by without noticing, oblivious to everything but the small miseries and joys to which the school day condemned them. I remembered that sensation from my own school years. I remembered the care I had to take, not to stand out among my classmates. I could have gone to another school, but Mother wanted me to stay close to home, which meant I had to attend the village school, with children who were poorer and less bright than I was. It was an effort not to become a target, especially with the older boys. But I managed quite well. I never put myself forward, never volunteered; in games, I waited to be chosen, in class I waited to be asked. I always seemed to do my best, but I was careful to get the odd question wrong, to seem foolish on occasion, to let the others laugh at me from time to time. I thought I was being smart, but now I see that it was so easy to behave that well because I felt nothing but contempt for most of my classmates.

The one exception was a boy in my class called Alexander. He was locked into a shell of isolation: because he was deaf, his speech seemed odd and amusing to the other children. All the teachers treated him with a special, condescending kindness, which he obviously hated. I made some efforts to become his friend, with almost no success. He regarded everyone with suspicion. Sometimes I would see him, out in the fields, standing with his head thrown back, staring up into the sky, as if he could see something there that nobody else could detect. I wondered what it was like to live like that. I had imagined that deaf people were locked into a calm and steady silence, but when I looked it up in a book, I discovered there was noise inside their heads, monotonous and ugly, like the space between channels on the radio. I wanted to ask Alexander how he thought: if he could see the words, instead of hearing them, whether he thought in words at all, or whether there were long gaps in his mind, when absence took over. I know, for certain, that he was looking for something. He would find telegraph poles and stand with his arms wrapped around them, his chest and face pressed to the wood, as if he could feel or hear something, coursing through the wires. Maybe he could. If I could have had a friend in school, it would have been him. If I could have asked one question, I would have asked Alexander what it was like to be how he was, but I imagine he would have found it impossible to answer.

Mostly, I was alone. At lunch-time, I would sit in the library with my favourite book. I remember it clearly, even now: it was called *The Junior Dictionary Illustrated*. The cover showed a girl lying on the grass in summer, reading, and an ideal schoolmaster handing a book to an ideal boy, while another girl stood by, holding her own book like a pet or a baby. The first page bore the legend '*We Live in a World of Words*', and showed a variety of objects in boxes, with captions for their names, and the country in which the names had originated: *bantam* and *tattoo*, from the South Seas; *rose* and *mutton* from France, *bungalow* and *jungle* from India, *marmalade* and *cobra* from Portugal. I loved that book. I loved its pictures of rhododendrons and rabbits, and perfect children skating on perfect ice rinks. I loved its simple definitions, the sense it gave that everything could be classified and explained, and I took what it said at face value: we live in a world of words, things exist because of language, and language could as easily change things as keep them fixed in place.

Mother drove me to school in the mornings. In that school no one else travelled by car, and it set me apart from the others to glide by, and have them see me, sitting in the front alongside a woman who was always expensively dressed and utterly remote. Every now and then she took it into her head to offer a lift to some child who took her fancy, which only made things more awkward. After school, I insisted on walking home by myself. It was nearly three miles, but the road was straight and there was little traffic. It ran out of the village past the houses, skirted a row of allotments, then passed a farm. The farm always seemed deserted: I remember the yard, and a grey metal hopper blotted with rust, tilted over a hedge like a shipwreck. Sometimes a herd of muddy, black-haired cattle stood by the fence, watching me pass; sometimes a dog ran to the gate and barked, but mostly the yard was empty, a pile of logs against the barn, an old tractor marooned in a pool of weeds, rusted remains of farm machinery propped against the walls, like the remnants of a forgotten civilisation.

In winter it would be almost dark by the time I reached the farm. For the next mile, there was nothing but fields on both sides. The silence was heavy and thick, like velvet, broken only by an occasional splash in the ditch beside the road, or a car swishing by on its way to Weston. There were no lights on that stretch of road, but that did not bother me till I got to Laurel Cottage, about half a mile from home. I never saw lights at Laurel Cottage, but I knew the foreign woman was there, watching me the way she did in the summertime. That bothered me. The people in the village said the foreign woman was mad. Nobody knew how she lived. Sometimes she would be sitting in her garden when I passed by, and she would be knitting, or reading a book. People who had seen inside the cottage said she had hundreds of books, all piled on the floor in the sitting room. Once I saw her standing at her door, eating an apple, and I plucked up the courage to say good afternoon. She looked at me and smiled, but she did not reply. I was intensely curious about her. I wanted to know where she had come from, and what it was that had made her mad.

She wasn't mad all the time. The people in the village said she took fits because of something that had happened to her in the war. I had seen her myself, on occasion, standing in her garden, talking to the trees, when the fit was on her. She would walk round in circles, talking in some language that no one else understood. At first I thought it was Polish or German, because people in the village said she had come from Germany as a refugee after the war. Later, Mother told me it was not a real language at all, but something the woman had invented. As far as I knew, she only ever spoke this language to the trees in her garden.

Her fits would last for hours at a time. To begin with, she seemed excited, even happy: she walked quickly around the garden, sometimes reaching out and brushing a tree with her fingers as she passed. She would talk constantly in a kind of singsong – there was no structure, no syntax. The words seemed to merge, one into another, yet there was no doubt that they meant something to her, that she intended something by them. Then, about an hour after she began, her voice would change. Now there were spaces between one word and the next, everything began to collapse inward, into a kind of slow motion. Eventually she turned her back on the tree she had been talking to, and walked away. Whenever that happened, she always looked disappointed, as if she had failed in some task. Once, when I was out hunting for animals, I hid in a bush near the cottage and watched the whole thing. It was beautiful in its way, and I was curious about her private language. I wanted to know what it meant to her, what it was she thought she was saying.

Once I was walking home in the springtime. It was late afternoon, still light; the rain had been falling all day, heavy and loud on the windows at school. Now it had stopped but the fields and gardens were still wet. The world seemed abnormally still, after the violence of the rain. As I approached Laurel Cottage, I thought I saw something move – or rather, I had the feeling that someone, some person had moved a moment before I looked, and was now standing amongst the bushes, hushed, waiting for me to pass. Nothing was visible, but I had that sensation you sometimes get, playing hide and seek, when someone gives himself away by trying too hard to stay hidden. I knew it was not an animal I sensed there, but a human being, though I could not have said why. Then, just as I reached the front gate, the foreign woman stepped out from amongst the leaves and stood there, stark naked, streaming with rainwater, and laughing softly to herself. She was so close I could almost have touched her. She was looking straight at me, but I do not think it was me she saw. She was playing a game with someone else, perhaps with someone who had died years before, or it might have been someone she had invented, but it was not me.

I had never seen a naked woman. She was thin, but her breasts and hips were large, and the sight of her thick, dark pubic hair excited and frightened me. I could not take my eyes off her.

As we stood there, face to face, I had the idea of touching her wet skin, of stroking the hair, but I hurried on, walking backwards so I could still see her, afraid to turn my back on her white body.

I waited outside Mrs Olerud's house for three hours. It's strange, how a neighbourhood changes when the people leave. A silence falls; the arrival of a delivery van becomes an event; animals appear and move through the gardens in virtual slow motion. It always seems something has just happened, moments before, but when you look there is nothing.

I didn't notice the boy at first. Like one of the animals, he seemed to emerge from nowhere. I hadn't seen the front door open, but he might have come from the back of the house. He was standing on the path, looking towards the end of the road, as if he was expecting someone. I was sure he hadn't seen me. I got out of the car, clutching my bouquet of flowers, and walked over to the gate.

'Hello, Jeremy,' I said.

He looked angry. It was obvious that he remembered who I was and didn't want to admit it.

'Is your mother home?' I asked.

He moved his head almost imperceptibly. I leaned down to open the gate and he retreated a few steps, holding his arms out, as if he could prevent me from entering by sheer willpower. I noticed he was holding something in his left hand.

'What have you got there?' I asked.

He looked at his hand. It was shaped in a loose fist, cradling something that must have been breakable, or precious to him. Slowly his face broke into a half-smile. He took three steps forward, looked up at me and, holding out his hand, turned it over and unclenched his fingers, like a conjuror performing a trick.

He was holding a baby mouse. It was tiny, almost bald, and quite motionless.

'It's a mouse,' I said, in my best adult-to-child voice. He gave me a look of contempt. He didn't want my kindness. Showing me the mouse had been some kind of trick on his part, some act of deception he alone understood. I held out my hand.

'Shall I take it now?' I asked him.

He pulled away his hand and stepped back.

'But it's dead,' I said softly.

He shook his head.

'You know it is,' I said. 'It was only a baby. You should have left it in the nest.'

I thought he would cry. His expression showed that I was responsible for the death, that the mouse would have remained alive, warmed in his clenched hand for hours, if I hadn't turned up, to tell him otherwise. He lifted the animal to his face, and stroked the naked body against his cheek. Then he turned, ran back across the lawn and vanished around the corner of the house.

I had no intention of following. I pushed open the gate and walked in. Now I could see that the front door was open, and slightly ajar. It might have been like that all morning, but when I knocked nobody answered.

I walked around the side of the house to look for the boy. The garden at the back was dark, overgrown with deep weeds, the kind that ran and trailed through the trees, old man's beard, bryony with its red, venomous-looking berries, tall stands of dock and nightshade along the fence. It was still wet. The sun hadn't risen high enough over the roofs to penetrate this far and, even if it had, the air here was dark and heavy and it was probably never dry at the far end, where it had once been planted with shade-loving plants, aucuba and holly and elaeagnus. I felt that, if I walked to the end of the path, I could disappear, just as the child had done. I couldn't see him but I knew he was there, crouched in the centre of his own private wilderness, watching me.

The back door was wide open, but I was certain he hadn't gone inside. He belonged to the garden, not the house. I had a momentary image of him hunting for small rodents and insects, his fingers and mouth caked with fresh soil, mouse bones cracking between his teeth.

I thought of leaving. Then it occurred to me that something might have happened to Mrs Olerud. She had seemed on edge the previous evening, almost despairing at times; now the thought passed through my mind that she might have done something to harm herself. A few days before, on the radio, I'd heard how a couple had committed suicide in a holiday cottage in Wales. They had killed themselves with alcohol and sleeping pills and their two children, aged four and eighteen months, had been left alone with the bodies, too frightened to go out. It had been several days before anybody noticed something was wrong. When the police forced their way into the cottage, they found the children in the kitchen, huddled together behind the door. They had been living on corn flakes.

I stepped into the kitchen and looked around. No one was there. I called out. Nobody answered. When I went through to the sitting room, I found Mrs Olerud, laid out on the sofa, in a floral-patterned dressing gown. She appeared to be asleep, or perhaps unconscious. On the coffee table, a bottle of gin, a glass, still half-full, a large plastic bottle of tonic, now empty, were the only objects that looked out of place in the clean, well-ordered room. I glanced at the clock on the mantelpiece; it was eleven thirty. Lying there, with one arm raised, half-covering her face, Mrs Olerud was obviously drunk. The dressing gown was covered in large, dark flowers, it reminded me of something Mother had worn, years before, on summer afternoons; as far as I could tell, the woman was naked under the thin satin. I stood over her. She looked impossibly moist and soft; I could see her breathing and I imagined how warm she would be if I touched her, how smooth the skin would be on her neck and shoulders. The dressing gown was knotted loosely at the waist with a wide belt, in the same red and white material; it had fallen open just above the knee, where her legs were bent slightly; though her arm was raised to half-cover her face, I could see her mouth, and I was tempted to run my fingers over her full, red lips. I was struck again by how beautiful she looked; for a moment I was almost overcome by a feeling akin to grief, a mixture of longing and despair that surprised me. I set the flowers down carefully on the edge of the coffee table.

'Mrs Olerud?'

I stood waiting for her to respond; then, when she made no move, I sat down on the floor next to the sofa and rested my fingers, gently, on her ankle. I could not see her eyes, but I could tell she wasn't so much asleep as unconscious. Her breathing was slow and shallow, somehow academic, like the breathing of an automaton, like the waxwork Sleeping Beauty I had once seen in a museum. I slid my hand lightly along her leg, past the knee, to where the thigh filled out, smooth and warm to the touch. I was excited. Looking at her like this, at rest, I could see she was all roundness, perfect in proportion, and I wanted to touch her everywhere at once, to have a thousand hands, to explore and describe the entire surface of her body. At the same time, the idea began to form in my mind that she was not unconscious at all; or at least, that she was half-aware of what was happening, and was only pretending she was asleep, to see what I would do next. I lifted my hand gently – it seemed what might disturb her, or make her take fright, wasn't so much the moment of contact, as the moment's withdrawal – and I found where the belt was knotted around her waist. She lay still. I teased the knot loose, slowly, taking pleasure in the way I was able to contain my desire, then I let the belt fall and turned back the gown so her hips and breasts were naked. I bent towards her. I could feel the warmth off her body; I could smell that sweet mustiness of sleep, mingled with her perfume. I could almost taste her hair, her wet mouth, the salt of her skin. Her breasts were a little smaller than I would have expected, and her belly was a little rounded; she had an old-fashioned body, like the figure of Eve in one of those medieval paintings that showed the Expulsion from Eden. I ran a fingertip along her arm. It was soft, warm, covered in fine down. Still she did not move. I reached out and stroked her softly, running my fingers lightly over her breasts, belly and hips. I was afraid she would wake at any moment; at the same time, I wanted her to know I was there, to respond, to pull me towards her, into the moist warmth of her flesh.

Suddenly I was aware of something and turned. The boy, Jeremy, was standing in the kitchen doorway, watching me. I hadn't heard him come in; he was quite still, quite silent, and I realised he'd been standing there for some time, literally holding his breath, curious to see what I would do. That was what I'd heard – that soft intake of breath – though something else was suggested, a slight turn of the head, as he scented the air, like an animal. Yes, that was it, he was scenting me, taking me in fully, perhaps for the first time. Now, seeing that I'd noticed he was there, he smiled, softly, conspiratorially. I pulled back the hem of the dressing gown and stood up. I thought he would run to his mother and wake her, but all he did was stand there, frowning slightly, disappointed, or puzzled by something, as if I had just given him some task to perform that he did not understand. I noticed that his hair and clothes were wet, and his hands were dirty, crusted at the knuckles with scabs of loam, as if he had just been digging.

'It's all right,' I said. 'She's only sleeping.'

I was aware of the defensiveness in my voice, the note of guilt, and it irritated me, that I had felt the need to explain myself to a child. Yet there was no sign that he understood, either what I had said, or what he had caught me doing. I backed away from the sofa, towards the door that led to the hallway.

'I'd better go,' I said. 'I'll call back later. When she's awake.'

He shook his head fiercely, like a dog, scattering drops of water everywhere. Then he turned and ran out, leaving a trail of muddy footprints across the kitchen floor. Mrs Olerud stirred then, or perhaps she only moved in her sleep, and I left quickly, leaving the front door ajar, just as I'd found it. As I walked away, I had the idea that I knew her in a way she would understand the next time she saw me, like the idea that sometimes comes when you touch someone in a dream then see them the next day, on the street, or in a shop, and you're sure they remember the same dream, the one they had the night before, where you touched them and they responded, surprised by their own complicity, amazed by a moment of unexpected surrender. At the same time, I felt Mrs Olerud had intended it that way, that she had somehow contrived the whole thing.

I returned at precisely two o'clock on Saturday afternoon, as we had agreed. Once again, Mrs Olerud was dressed impeccably, and she was as remote and polite as she had been at our first meeting. Yet the thought remained that she half-remembered everything that had happened, that a secret complicity existed between us. Once again, I brought her flowers: before I arrived

I had half-expected her to refuse them, but she accepted the gift naturally, and carried the bouquet into the kitchen, to put it in water. I noticed, then, that the flowers I had brought on my previous visit were standing on a shelf to one side of the fireplace, carefully arranged in a bright-blue ceramic vase. At that moment, I knew Mrs Olerud had been aware of me the previous day. She had allowed me to touch her, to explore her skin, and there was no doubt in my mind that she would have allowed me to go further. The flowers were a signal of that fact.

On this occasion, however, we were polite and formal. We discussed the weather. Mrs Olerud served me tea, as she had on my first visit, apologising again that she had no milk, and asking if lemon would do. There was a ritual quality in everything she did, as if she had to perform every action exactly as she had always done. She served tea as if enacting a ceremony, as if she were Japanese; every movement was controlled, every word, no matter how trivial, seemed calculated. It was as if she was afraid of letting something slip, of giving something away. When it came time to fetch Jeremy, she managed to conceal her anxiety, and he was produced from upstairs, like an exhibit in a museum. As on my first visit, he was clean and well-dressed enough, but now he was sleepy, almost groggy, as if he had been drugged. He seemed not to recognise me, and showed no signs of the wildness I had seen in him before. I tried half-heartedly to attract his attention – I knew by now that he understood what I was saying – but he remained withdrawn and, after about ten minutes, his mother led him away. I was mystified. Mrs Olerud appeared to be entirely in control of her strange child, yet she could not quite hide her fear of him. I had seen evidence of a near-animal quality in his behaviour, but that could easily have been the result of loneliness or neglect, and it certainly wasn't enough to explain her discomfort. Was she afraid the child would harm her in some way? Or was she afraid of what she might do to him?

When she returned, we sat a while, making small talk. I was beguiled by her beauty, just as I was bored by our conversation. She asked about my interest in what she called 'speech therapy' and I explained as well as I could. Occasionally we lapsed into silence and I sat watching her, looking for any sign she might offer, that she remembered the events of the previous day. I knew she did, but she gave nothing away, and after what felt like a respectable time, I left. As before, she stopped me at the door; this time her suggestion that I visit her again was almost casual. I immediately agreed, and we set a date for the following week. I knew she understood that I would come before then, that I would not be able to stay away so long. There was a promise between us, even if nothing was said.

This pattern established itself over the next several visits. On some days, I would arrive in the morning and find her in a kind of trance, wandering about the house in her floral-patterned gown, or lying on the sofa, as if waiting for me to find her there. Sometimes she had been drinking, but not always. Sometimes the child would be playing in the garden; often he was nowhere to be seen. I would knock at the front door, and she wouldn't answer; then I would walk around the side of the house and go in through the kitchen, carrying whatever gift I had brought, a bunch of flowers, a box of chocolates, a bottle of wine. The first few times this happened, I tried talking to her, asking where Jeremy was, and if she was all right, but her only response was to wait, silently, while I loosened her belt and slipped back her dressing gown. Her eyes would be closed, but she wasn't sleeping, and I was certain she was aware of everything that was happening.

Her body was astonishing. She was always damp, very warm – as if feverish – yet she smelled sweet, and her skin was smooth to the touch, almost incredibly soft. When I kissed her, her mouth would be very wet. Sometimes I would have her on the sofa, in the sitting room, with the back door open and the child somewhere outside. I wondered what he understood, if he knew I was there, if he was watching. Sometimes I would force her on to the floor and take her violently – there was something in her passivity that demanded it – and it gave me pleasure then, to think that the boy might see. I would raise her legs and bend back her knees, so I could pin her down and drive into her. I did whatever I liked: she was always utterly compliant, lying with her face pressed to the floor, sometimes crying out or moaning softly, plaintive, and oddly childlike. Sometimes I had to go looking through the house before I found her. Once, she was lying face down on the bed, and she did not move or make a sound all the time I was there. It was like having sex with a corpse – yet I was certain she was aware of me, and of what I was doing. No matter how I found her, no matter what I did, she never spoke, except to utter those odd little sounds. When I was finished, I left her and went home without a word, with her smell on me, warm and sweet, like a mingling of honey and blood. Every time I went to her house I was excited: I wanted her so violently it was almost painful, and taking her was a mixture of pleasure and exquisite relief.

Afterwards, though, I would feel slightly disgusted, as if I had been exposed to some kind of contamination, as if I had deliberately allowed myself to be sullied. There were days when I was angry with her, for being so powerless, so available; yet on the other days, when she would be fully-dressed, formal, almost excessively polite, pretending nothing had ever happened between us, I wanted to pull her to the floor and take her by force. I might have had her the day before, there might still be bruises under her clothes, but she acknowledged nothing. We would sit in the living room, drinking tea, then she would fetch Jeremy, and I would offer him little gifts, to win his trust, to break through his suspicion, though by now I was only going through the motions. The child accepted the bribes, but he gave no sign that he recognised the giver. Mrs Olerud – I always called her Mrs Olerud, never Karen, though I knew that was her name – would encourage him, trying to make him open up, as if I were a doctor, or an expert of some kind, come to administer a cure. If anything, this assistance was counterproductive: Jeremy seemed to regard her with as much suspicion as he showed me. He was never badly behaved. He came when he was called, and stood stock-still while I talked to him; he ate the sweets I brought him, one after another, though with no sign of pleasure. He wasn't really there; perhaps he was nothing more than the alert animal he seemed, at home in the wet undergrowth of the garden, like some wolf child. He was fascinating to watch, in his state of limbo, utterly incommunicado, but I knew, no matter what I did, I would never understand him. I kept going back, but not to see him. I wanted those mornings when Karen Olerud was lost in her trance, naked under her dressing gown, waiting for me, or for some imagined other, whose place I was assuming, briefly, without acknowledgement.

Certain rules were understood. As soon as I had finished with her, I knew I had to go. I would dress quickly and leave the way I had come, without a backward glance. I knew I should not talk to her, as if she were a sleepwalker who must not be wakened. I could do anything I wanted, as long as I did not talk. I also knew that it was part of her game that I must never speak about or show any sign of remembering what happened between us on the trance days. It was a ghost life she had. I was using her, but she was also using me. It was her privilege to invent the rules: they were in place before I even arrived on the scene. I simply followed them. I might have been taking part in a ritual she had evolved with her husband, or some other man she had known; I might have been fulfilling a fantasy she had built up, over years of isolation. At the time, I didn't care. In spite of everything, in spite of the moments of self-disgust I felt, when I drove home with her smell on me, I wanted her.

One afternoon, I found her naked on her bed. She had been drinking; she did not move when I lay down beside her; she did not respond when I began moving inside her, and I became more and more excited. Her passivity enraged me at such moments. I was convinced she knew I was there, and I was trying to provoke her, to make her acknowledge me, but nothing I did made any difference – she lay still, silent, motionless.

Finally I must have fallen asleep beside her, though only for a matter of minutes. When I woke I was aware of a sensation, something like a memory, though it was a memory I couldn't place: a mingling of warmth and scent and a faint biscuity smell, a feeling of utter detachment, as if nothing could ever matter: nothing that had ever happened, nothing that was happening now, nothing that might happen in the future. But it was more than that. The sensation I was experiencing was more than the sum of its parts. I looked at Karen Olerud and I felt a surge of violence and desire. I wanted to possess her, once and for all; I wanted to split her body open and suck out her essence; I wanted to drink her, to assume her. She lay with her arms by her side and her legs apart, like a doll that someone had dropped there, as if she couldn't have moved of her own volition. She seemed to be asleep now. I moved over to her, and slipped my hand between her legs. She was still wet. I raised the hand to my face and sniffed; the smell was so sweet, so unlike any other, and I was certain, if I could have peeled away the surface she would smell like that inside, everywhere I touched and tasted. I parted her legs and moved inside her. I wanted to have sex with her one last time, then, as I was coming, I would cover her face with the pillow and hold it down, feeling her struggle for life then give up and fade away, while I moved inside her. I felt certain that, if I did so, something would be released, something I could take into myself.

She was still sleeping. As I raised the pillow, she stirred and turned her head; at the same time, I became aware of a noise, like someone banging softly and repetitively somewhere in the house. It was a moment before I came to my senses. I wanted to go on moving, to finish what I had started, but I was afraid Mrs Olerud would wake up, or Jeremy would come running into the room and find us. I hadn't seen him earlier, when I'd sneaked in through the back door. I had assumed he was outside, playing in the garden, crouched under a shrub or crawling through the weeds along the fence, hunting for mice. Now he must have come inside. The bedroom door was still open – perhaps he had climbed the stairs and seen us, naked on his mother's bed. Perhaps he had hurt himself and was trying to attract attention, lying in the hallway with both legs broken, banging his hand against the baluster.

As I dressed, the noise stopped. I walked to the far end of the landing. the child's door was open, but the room was empty. Then, after a moment, the banging began again, a little louder than before. It was coming from downstairs, from the kitchen. I hurried down.

Jeremy was sitting on the floor, surrounded by food – sliced bread, bright puddles of orange juice, cuts of meat oozing water and thin blood. The fridge was open; it appeared that he had just sat down and pulled out everything he could reach, scattering it around him, rolling bottles across the floor, letting the cartons burst as they fell. It was warm, and the fridge had already begun to defrost; I could see fish on a willow-pattern plate, in a pool of rimy water, splashes of yoghurt, trickles of thaw on the bottles and jars. Now he was banging a tub of margarine on the wet lino, splashing milk and fruit juice and meltwater all over his face and clothes.

'What are you doing?' I said.

He looked up at me. His face was a blur of grease and blood, and I realised he had been eating raw food off the floor, gouging out handfuls of butter and meat from their containers, lapping up the spilt milk.

'You were hungry,' I said, more to myself than to him.

He made a soft snuffling noise, and pointed at the midden on the floor. He looked like an animal. Once again, I was struck by the thought that he didn't belong in a house. He should have been kept out of doors, digging for grubs and worms in the shrubbery, sucking the matter out of birds' eggs. At the very least, he should have been kept in a pen, in one of those wire runs for rabbits and chickens.

I watched, as he lowered his face and began lapping up orange juice from a puddle on the lino, and it occurred to me, then, that the boy was acting: he knew exactly what he was doing, and he was doing it for effect, just as his mother knew what she was doing, when she sat naked in her bedroom, swigging gin and waiting for me to arrive. Now, all of a sudden, I was tired of these games. I was tired of the child, and of his comatose mother; I was tired of the ornaments, the silver frames, the floral dressing gown. I was tired of the whole affair. I turned to go and that was when I saw the knife, the smallest glimmer at the edge of my vision, an apparition of silver through the litter of broken eggs and bloodstains. The boy almost caught me with it, slashing at my leg with a sudden, neat swing of the arm. I managed to twist away and turn, as he came again, reaching out, snatching his hand in mid-air, more by luck than by judgement. For a moment I looked at his face in surprise; I expected a signal of some kind, a flicker at least of anger or hatred, but there was nothing. I held on to his hand as I twisted the knife loose and let it fall. The child's face was empty: there was nothing there, no fear in his eyes, just as there had been no anger. He simply gazed at me, coldly, and I knew his attempt to cut me had been a deliberate, calculated act. I held him tightly, locking his forearm in my fist.

I remembered all the times he had stood watching me, while I talked to him, or offered him sweets; watching me, like some animal from the woods, puzzled by the very fact of my existence. I realised then that he had been watching me all along: even when I hadn't seen him, he'd been there. He must have felt betrayed when he'd seen his mother pull me down on to the sofa, when he'd seen us disappear into her room. He must have listened to her little cries and whimpers and wondered what I was doing to her, and now he was trying to take his revenge. He hadn't lost his head for a moment; he had worked out a plan of sorts and set a trap for me. I smiled.

'You're quite clever, really,' I said. 'You're not as stupid as you pretend.'

He watched me. I think I saw a flicker of contempt then, as if he had guessed what I was going to do before I even knew myself. If he had, he still wasn't afraid: he kept his eyes fixed on my face as I took his thumb in my left hand and, with an effort I found quite exhilarating, twisted it back and felt it snap.

His face showed the pain, but he made no sound. He didn't cry out, he didn't even struggle, he only whimpered a little, towards the end, as I broke each finger in turn, gripping his arm tightly and holding him up as he began to slump, his face white as death, his eyes glazed, his legs giving way beneath him, as if he were suffering from vertigo. When I had finished I let him fall, and he lay still in the puddles of orange juice and egg yolk. I believe he must have fainted. I stood over him, listening: there was no sound from upstairs, no sound except his breathing. For a moment I was dizzy with the sheer immediacy of it all – the sweet-sickly smell, the boy's gold hair, his broken fingers, the thought of the woman upstairs, still sleeping, warm and damp and vulnerable. The thought passed through my head that I might go back up and finish what I had begun, but I pulled myself together and left, slipping out the back way as always, moving invisibly through the garden and out into the gathering darkness.

I got home just after sunrise. I had been driving around for hours; now the light was like silt on the walls, building up then shifting softly, forming slowly then crumbling away. The garden was still, but I could smell urine at the edge of the lawn, where a fox had come in through a gap in the wall. The shadows were deep, black and substantial, like blankets stacked under the pear trees and cotoneasters; the sun was already bright, but these dark patches would stay for hours, like trapdoors into a night that would never wholly dissolve, some limbo that was cold and damp and incomprehensible. I opened the back door and paused as something fluttered away – only a leaf, and not what it might have been, not the ghost I hoped for every time I returned. I passed on through the hall and into the kitchen, looking for a sign of that otherlife the house contained whenever I was away, but all I found was the table spotted with crumbs and the cups and plates stacked on the draining board, just as I'd left them. Sometimes, coming home in the early morning like this, I'd imagine things had altered while I was absent: a knife on the bread board that I didn't remember leaving out, a book face down on the table, a cup brimming with tea and dishwater in the sink. The evidence I wanted didn't need to be too elaborate or detailed. I could have constructed an entire afterlife from a half-moon of lemon rind or a small blister of jam on the tablecloth. It would have taken so little to convince me that Mother was still in the house; that, even if I could never see her, she resumed possession of this space when I was gone, fingering the spines of her favourite books in the library, or sitting in the conservatory, drinking tea in the dawn light, the way she'd always done when she couldn't sleep. In spite of her death, in spite of the fact that I can never find evidence of her continued presence, Mother is still the only person who is completely real for me. In life she had been bound to the fabric of the house, wearing into it, taking on the same colours and textures, like those prints on the walls and the curtains she'd hung years before as a young bride, fading imperceptibly in the sunlight, becoming subtler, assuming an evenness of tone, a homogeneous quality.

I made a pot of coffee. I couldn't eat, and I felt anxious, as if there was something I'd missed, something important that I'd failed to take into account. I was trying to work out what it was, to pin it down – I was sure it had something to do with the boy – but instead of finding an answer, I kept returning to an image I had, something to do with a mouse, something to do with the kitchen, the early morning, the first sunlight. It took a while for the memory to form, then it became clear, though I couldn't see the connection with what had just happened. It had been years ago, when I was about eight or nine. It was just after breakfast; I must have been ill, or maybe it was just one of those days when Mother decided I didn't need to go to school, that she would set me some work herself. She had taken my things away and I was trying to read. I liked to sit at the dining room table to study, rather than the big desk in the library, where I couldn't see the garden. The books Mother gave me were difficult: she always set me tasks that were too advanced for my age, partly because she overestimated my ability, partly because she felt I needed to be pushed and challenged in order to grow. It was typical of her tangential generosity, this refusal to believe that I might be stumped and give up, and she was often right: no matter how difficult it was, I usually learned something new. It was a good feeling, sometimes, sitting at the wide table, bent to my studies, half-aware of something that began to materialise in the room whenever my attention was focused elsewhere, a form composed of scent and shadows, a presence I came to expect, created from the smells of cake and upholstery, from the spices on the kitchen shelves and the faint must of aspergillus in the books that had stood on the library shelves for years. This familiar of the house was elusive and mysterious, even a little sinister in the way it waited till everyone was occupied before it emerged, half-formed, into the light. As soon as I looked up, it would disappear, explaining itself away as it went. I would keep my head down, and try to become half-aware of it, without giving it my full attention, the way you try to look at something at the edge of your vision, knowing it will vanish if you focus. I liked knowing it was there. I liked having a secret and I liked the way it changed everything, how it revealed new details in the books I was reading: the skeletal diagrams of birds' wings and lizards, the names of polyhedrons and angles and the ages of geological time combined to form a vague text-book mass, part-algebra,

63

part-taxonomy, that loomed in my dreams whenever I fell asleep in the chair then woke again, only minutes later.

Maybe I had drifted off that morning, then started awake, not quite sure of where I was. All I remember is turning slightly and seeing the mouse – no form to begin with, only a slight, spastic motion at the edge of vision, the kind of small, almost involuntary movement that immediately captures your attention. It was as if the mouse had betrayed itself by its very desire for secrecy. I slid down from the chair and walked over to where it lay on its side, twitching and gazing up at me – its body was caught in the poison, the movements were quite automatic, quite involuntary. Only its eyes were alive. Mother had explained how such poisons worked: they destroyed the internal organs, and it took some time for the animal to die, as the liver broke down in a series of haemorrhages. The poison was designed that way, to provoke internal bleeding, and avoid mess. As I stooped, peering down at the thing, I was struck by the knowledge that, in spite of its pain, in spite of its near-paralysis, the mouse had not given up, it seemed unable to accept that death was inevitable. When Mother had told me that animals found quiet, unexposed places to die, I had always imagined they knew they were dying, and accepted it, almost gracefully. Now I saw that this wasn't so at all: they crept into corners in the hope of surviving, they only knew they were weakened and exposed, easy prey, and their instinct was to find a hidden place and try to outlive whatever it was they were suffering. It had been a mistake to imagine they wanted to be alone, to die in peace. Animals have no knowledge of death: for them, death is the unexpected end of life, something they resist by instinct, for no good reason. In that sense, their existence has an almost mechanical quality.

I stood there for some time, bent slightly towards the

mouse, trying to figure out how much it knew about what was happening, and whether it was aware of me. Most of all, I was waiting to see it die, to see what happened when the life seeped away; whether it was a gradual process, or if there was a moment when the animate thing became inanimate, when the light went out, as it were. It took a long time. It had probably been there for a while before I saw it; even so, it was still moving twenty minutes later, though by then there was a blankness in the eyes, a lack of awareness, that surprised me. I had imagined the body died first, then the mind faded away, glowing for a while like a cigarette butt as it burned out. Now it seemed that the mind was the first to go, and the body kept going, trying to hang on to something that wasn't there any more.

From that moment on, I lost interest in the road-kills and the dead birds I found in the woods. From that moment on, I wanted to study the living. There is something beautiful in the stillness of death, in its irreversibility. But, after a time, I wanted more than entry to a corpse. I wanted to open up the living creature, to see the heartbeat and how the blood worked; I wanted to act as witness and celebrant in a ceremony of some kind, to feel the pulse in the organs, to watch the life seep away in the eyes of my chosen subject. I believed there would be a moment when the spirit ebbed, and I wanted to know how that happened, how that moment looked. I wanted to see what it was like when the life dissolved, leaving nothing but inert matter.

It was a natural progression to substitute the living for the dead. Mother never found out what I was doing, of course; I kept these experiments secret, performing them in the woods, or in one of the abandoned barns further along the road, where the old Baker farm had been. To begin with I wasn't quite sure how to go about the dissections. I knew the mechanics, but I was shy of the live animals and birds I managed to capture.

I had fair success with the home-made traps I had learned to build from a book on taxidermy in the public library. I would set them up in the strip of woodland behind the house, then revisit them later, perhaps the same evening, or early the next morning, when nobody else was about. Often they were empty, but now and again I found a mouse or a vole, scrambling about in the little box, trying frantically to escape. Sometimes the animal was dead. If it was a bird, it might have damaged itself, the wings spread and tattered, the feathers ruined. I only caught birds once or twice, and I let them go immediately. The idea of dissecting a bird revolted me.

My first live dissection was a large mouse. The pleasure of opening it up, and knowing it was still alive, knowing the life was bleeding away through my fingers was almost overwhelming. I had studied methods of dissection in the library books: most concerned the opening of corpses for taxidermy, but one I had found in the biology section described in detail methods that could easily be adapted to living creatures: gross dissections, for larger animals, that could be performed with everyday kitchen knives; fine-scale dissections, for the removal or display of organs and glands, using mounted needles and fractured glass edges; and normal-scale dissections - involving everything from dogs to earthworms – which required scalpels, dissecting needles, forceps, blunt seekers and scissors – the kinds of tools that were easily found in a biology student's dissecting kit. It was no trouble to get my father to buy me a set. A few days after I made my request, the postman presented me with an elegant wooden box, which contained all the instruments I needed, and more. They were so beautiful, I would take them out and handle them for the sheer pleasure of it.

It took a great deal of practice to reach the point where I could open an animal and hold it a moment, before I felt its life seep away. Rabbits were best: they lasted longer, and they were easy to catch. As I worked, I experienced a higher form of grace, a plugging in to something, a connectedness, when the blood flowed back along the blade, seaming my fingers and palms, spilling out over the board and drying, the dark electricity bleeding away almost immediately, long before the organs darkened and congealed. Now I had it right, the meat parted cleanly from the bones, and there was something exciting in it all, like the shedding of a veil, an involuntary revelation. Pinned to the dissecting board, and drugged with spirits from my father's drinks cabinet, the animal barely struggled. I was touched by the strange gravity of the flesh; I was drawn in by a dark attraction, an interplay between my turning wrist and whatever it was – spirit, life, *élan vital* – that was suspended there. Sometimes I managed to open a living body carefully enough to be able to see the heart beating, to see the lungs still full of air, to see the feeling in the eyes. It lasted only a short time, but it was a near-perfect moment. Later, when I was disposing of the body, I would bury the animal behind the outhouse and lay a stone on the grave, as a mark of respect. It had given me something it could never have understood; for a moment, I had looked into life itself, and I knew that, one day, I would discover its essence.

I stayed at home for a long time. I didn't know if Karen Olerud would report me to the police. I thought she might not have done, to avoid embarrassing questions as to why I was in her house, but I couldn't know for sure. For weeks it felt as if time had stopped. The garden lay still and silent under a thick blanket of early snow, and the waiting made it worse, but nobody came and I was left alone. Everything was as it had always been: Mother's room locked and still, a virtual presence behind the door; the library full of books; the rack in the hall festooned with her coats and scarves. It was something I did, as the seasons changed: in summer I put out her shawl and the light raincoats she would wear for gardening; at the end of October, I'd carry out her heavy winter coats and scarves, and I'd leave her gloves on the shelf in the hall, as if she were still there, and might need them. I knew she was gone, but that was no reason to forget her. It was one form of afterlife, at least, her life in my mind, her existence preserved in small rituals and gestures. It was the one thing of which I could be sure. That and the weather. It's an odd thing, but I've always believed that the dead are somehow connected to the weather, as if they were the ones who made it snow, as if they were present, somehow, in those gusts of wind that blow in from the distance, seeking me out, like spirits trying to communicate.

It was the wettest summer in years, during those last few months when Mother was dying. She seemed to enjoy the damp weather; it was as if it sealed her off from the rest of the world, as if the village was further away than ever. When the rainfall was heavy and dark, we could barely see the end of the garden, much less the road and the fields beyond. Sometimes it rained all day and the quality of time changed: the secret life of the house was resumed, a slow life of sootfalls and woodlice and the possibility of ghosts on the stairs. Mother would ask me to prop her up in bed, and she would sit reading, sneaking glances at herself in the mirror when she thought I wasn't looking – watching herself die, I suppose. I believe she found the process interesting, even as it horrified her to observe the transformation from the woman she had been into the grotesque shadow she was becoming. I could see her noticing the changes in her appearance, but I felt obliged to act as if she simply had a bad cold, and I would come and go all day, bringing her books, bringing her tea and lemon biscuits and trays of sandwiches that she left to dry and curl on the bedside table. During the last several weeks, I had to help her to the bathroom, where she would wash carefully, then return, in her silk gown, to sit at the dressing table, choosing her perfume, applying a little make-up, combing her hair. I had to be careful not to look at her in the mirror, not to see what she was seeing. It was another fiction we created together. If I looked her straight in the face, I was looking at the woman she still felt she was, underneath the illness, but if I looked at her through the mirror, I was seeing the woman she saw: that worn, pinched face, her sunken eyes, the blackness around her mouth. I felt guilty when she caught my eye, as if I had deliberately betrayed her. To distract her attention, I would talk about the garden; the flowers that were still out, the birds I had seen in the apple tree.

I had never imagined Mother as a child till then. I had never thought about her as she was before she was married. The woman my father described in his stories seemed unreal to me, if only because Mother herself denied that woman's existence. But now she was dying, I was curious. I would ask her questions and sometimes she would answer; she was happy to talk about her childhood, or reminisce about times we'd had together. But she never spoke about the early years of her marriage. Mostly, her conversation consisted of vague, random memories, out of sequence and incomplete, so I never really knew how true it was. Nothing she told me felt any different from what I remembered of my own childhood; it was all part of the same continuum, snow in the woods, a hard, spare whiteness, a poignant sense of home, of its lights and warmth as illusory, or at best, irredeemably local. It was all sealed in the past, a purely mental phenomenon. I think she felt that too, and it troubled her. Meanwhile the doctor came and went, prescribing new drugs, stopping in the hall to make conversation and ask how I was – without a word, he had been forbidden to discuss this illness with me, just as I had been silently forbidden to ask him questions, or to express concern. Nothing would have offended Mother more than to have us talking in whispers outside the bedroom door, feeling sorry for her, admiring her courage, or plotting to put her in a hospital. It was hard to believe she was dying: it was her body that was ill, and it showed – black circles formed around her eyes, and her skin smelled darkly sweet, with a hint of softness, as if there was nothing there, under the surface, as if she would have collapsed inwards if I had touched her. But that was physical. I couldn't find it in my heart to believe her death would result in a complete annihilation; I think I accepted her body's death from the beginning, but there was another part of me that believed her mind, or her spirit, or something else that could not be defined, would never really end. Years before, she had begun paring down her life: she had barely spoken to my father in the two or three years before he died; later, she had become even more still and remote, as if she were enclosed in ice, or glass. In a matter of weeks, she severed all her connections. The people who had come to the house when my father was alive, people who had been her friends as well as his, were excluded now. They took it well; I imagine they thought she needed to be alone with her grief. But the truth was, she did not grieve. If anything, she seemed relieved at my father's sudden absence, as if it that was what she had been waiting for all her life. What she wanted was to be alone, to strip away everything that had accumulated over years of marriage and social life. By the time she became ill, she had condensed herself into an essence, and it seemed to me impossible that this essence could be lost.

During the illness, we developed a routine. I would bring flowers in from the garden; I would set pitchers of iced water by the bed, bowls of fruit, each day's selection of the books I thought she might want. I would rise early, take her breakfast up, help her to wash, then clear away her things while she put on her make-up. I understood that I had to be very businesslike in the mornings. The process had to vary as little as possible, otherwise the illness might have forced us into awkward moments of physical intimacy that we would both have found quite unbearable. We talked a good deal while all this was going on: we played games with one another, making puns, telling lies, referring to ourselves in the third person, anything to create a space, to resist the force that was pushing us together. Still, I had to be quick. Mother was always a very fastidious person – that was the quality I most admired in her – and I knew what torture it was for her, to be handled, even by me, to be washed, to be *physical*. I would leave her for an hour or so before lunch – our days were structured around meal-times, though neither of us ate very much – then I would carry trays up for us both and I'd sit opposite her, at the dressing table, remembering the times I had sat there as a child, watching her get dressed, admiring her perfumes. In those days we had played a different game with the mirror: the people in the glass were strangers, and we would talk to them, across one another, like conspirators, flirting with them lightly, the way married people sometimes flirt with strangers at a party, testing themselves, always keeping one eye on their real partners. I missed that time, but I never tried to revive it: the mirror was dangerous ground now, and we worked around its silvery field, as if it were some trap, waiting for us in the corner of the room.

As the summer advanced, we spent all our time in that one space. I began to feel we were being laced together by the sticky-sweet fabric of death that had begun to form. Our conversations, our carefully measured gestures and movements had become seamless. There was no longer any telling us apart. At night, when I went back to my own room, I could still feel her there, in the darkness, and the world outside was suspended, silent, like a closed cinema. By the end, I was afraid of becoming too accustomed to our mingled warmth and smell, of waking at exactly the same moment she woke, knowing what she wanted, of hearing her voice, even before she spoke. It was as if the cocoon that was being spun around her for some absurd and elaborate transformation had accidentally included me. There was even a complicity with the process in the house itself: objects became part of the event, the Chinese bowls in the hall, the books in the library, the boxes of glass and tinsel in the attic, the cutlery in the kitchen drawers – everything seemed brighter and heavier, more fixed, like pieces in a game of chess or the instruments of an arcane ritual. When I was alone, preparing meals or passing the time while she slept, I felt part of a process that had become irreversible. It felt as if I were being sealed up with her, that we were being laid down, like fossils, compressed under centuries of water and silt, compressed and simplified, reduced to our basic forms.

For some weeks, she deteriorated quietly. We continued as well as we were able, ignoring what we could. One afternoon I left her sleeping and went for a walk in the woods. I hadn't been out of the house in days and the fresh air was an exquisite and guilty pleasure. I didn't go far; I would never be more than a half-mile's walk from the house. It was a warm day, and I followed an old route, stopping in some of the places where we'd made our most interesting finds. I couldn't have been gone for more than an hour, but when I returned, the downstairs study was a mess: there was a broken bowl on the floor, several books had been pulled from their shelves, one of the candlesticks on the mantelpiece had fallen into the hearth. I thought someone had come in, and I ran upstairs to see if Mother was all right. She was lying on the floor next to the bed, clutching a book; when I went to lift her, there was an odd biscuity smell on her dressing gown. She was asleep, or unconscious. I got her on to the bed and covered her up. Her face was damp; her body smelled sweet and floury still but underneath there was a current of something else, the kind of warm smell you get in a pet shop or a zoo, a subtle mingling of egg and spoor. It wasn't exactly unpleasant, but it bothered me, and I felt it was a sign of something, the first indication of a new state of being, an eventual transformation.

She slept a long time and when she woke she looked much worse. All of a sudden, death was fully present in the room and it couldn't be ignored any longer. Until that moment, I had failed to register what was going on. I had imagined her changing, becoming someone new, or exchanging presence for some subtler state, but from that day on the smell of death became stronger, till it filled the room, tainting the water in her jug, bleeding into the sheets. I brought fresh flowers every morning: all the petals had fallen by the middle of the afternoon. From now on, too, she was in visible pain. For the first time, in utter bewilderment, I considered killing her. I had read about mercy killings and I did not want to be found wanting, if that was what she required. I watched her closely for any sign of an appeal; it would have taken no more than a word or a gesture for me to have placed a pillow over her face and held it down till she stopped breathing. But she gave no signal. Some part of her, I am sure, was appalled at the way her body kept on living, unable to let go, like all those animals I had watched as a child, her eyes fixed on something beyond me, something I could not see.

One morning, as I was clearing her breakfast things away, she pointed at the mirror.

'Cover it now,' she said. Her voice was still alive, still clear, the only part of her being that had remained undiminished.

I stared at her in surprise.

'I don't want to see myself like this,' she said. She was cool; as usual, she showed no emotion. 'Cover it up.'

I shook my head.

'You look fine,' I said. 'You're just tired today.'

She smiled.

'I'm tired every day,' she replied. 'Cover it up. I want to think of myself as I am. Not like that.'

I nodded.

'All right,' I said. 'I'll do it now.'

I carried her tray down and took some twine from the cupboard under the stairs; then I found an old shawl, and used it to cover the mirror, binding it with the twine, unable to shake the idea that we were still there, frozen on the surface of the glass, in a last glance. Now the room was darker; perhaps it was this dimming of the light that effected the change, but from that day on, she began to slide, losing touch with me, drifting in and out of something that resembled sleep, but was heavier and less permeable. I'd sit by the bed and watch her. She was already becoming hazy, less clearly defined; as she slept, I could feel her seeping away.

The last thing I remember clearly was the morning of the day she died. She had been asleep for a long time – or rather, she had been floating under the surface of the drugs the doctor had left for her, floating free like an underwater swimmer, drifting with the tide, becoming the current. Suddenly she opened her eyes and looked at me. Sometimes, when she woke from the drugs, she seemed surprised to see me, as if she couldn't quite work out who I was. But that day, she knew me immediately; she reached out her hand and brushed my forearm, as if she was trying to get my attention.

'Tell him when you see him,' she said, in a clear voice, without the least trace of a slur.

I nodded.

'Tell who, Mother?' I asked.

She shook her head.

'Just tell him,' she repeated. Then she made a sound – a kind of sob, though it was more than that, more deliberate, almost articulate, like a word in some foreign language that I didn't understand, rooted in some dark, wet place, the beginning of decay perhaps, the beginning of annihilation. Whatever it was, it transcended the woman I knew. There was nothing personal here. She tried to pull herself up, but she couldn't; a moment later she cried out, twisting her body round in an effort to shake herself free. She lay like that for minutes, it seemed, straining to be loosed from something – and I couldn't do anything, I couldn't act, I simply watched till she collapsed back and dwindled into absence.

It was eleven o'clock. I pulled the sheet up over her face, and went outside. I stood in the hall for several minutes, trying to decide what to do, then I went out for a walk. It was raining. The road to the village was covered with dark, oily puddles, and the cattle in the fields stood huddled for shelter under an oak tree. I didn't see anyone on the road and, for a moment, I felt certain that Mother and I were the last people in the world. I walked as far as the edge of the village, letting the rain trickle through my hair and run down my face, cleansing me of something, of some last vestige of ordinary being. When I got back it was lunch-time. I changed into dry clothes, then made some sandwiches and took them upstairs, with a glass of milk and an apple, to keep Mother company.

Late that afternoon I drew the curtains and sat beside her in silence. I caught myself listening, as if I imagined she would speak, as if she would resume one of her stories from years before, in that tone of voice she had when she had been obliged to break off, when my father had come in and interrupted her, or the telephone had called her downstairs – the tone of voice that told me the story was infinitely repeatable, that it could always be resumed, in exactly the same place, and nothing could bring it to an end. The petals had fallen from the flowers I had set by the bed – they had been fresh the day before, now they were scattered across the table and the floor, still soft, still almost living.

When the time came, when I felt ready, I took off my clothes and draped them over the chair by the window. It was beginning to get dark. Mother lay still, the way I had arranged her, with her arms by her sides, the sheet pulled up now, over her face. I switched on the lamp so I could see the bottles on the dressing table, glittering in the gold light. Mother had built up this collection of perfumes over years: she had added new varieties as they came on to the market, but she had never finished anything, never thrown anything away. There were fragrances that had gone out of fashion years before I was born, as well as timeless classics that had never gone off the market. I had always been fascinated by that table. Once, when I was a child, she had found me there, in front of the mirror, my face dusted with powder, my mouth a gash of lipstick, splashing Chanel on my neck and wrists. I have no memory of that afternoon; she told me years later that I'd looked like a baby vampire, with blotches of lipstick glistening on my teeth, like fresh blood. She said she'd been surprised to see my reflection in the glass: by rights, there should have been nothing there, only a gap where my face should have been, a metaphysical absence.

Now I stood, naked, in front of the wrapped mirror. I picked up each bottle in turn and anointed my body, reading the labels and choosing each scent carefully – one for the crook of the elbow, another for the collarbone, yet another for the skin between the index finger and the thumb, or the angle of the knee. To begin with, I could smell each one distinctly, but after a while, they all blended one into another, with the warmth of my body, till I felt I myself would evaporate, becoming a scent, a pure vapour.

I lifted the sheet. Mother's face was quite discoloured now, and it seemed, already, that something was missing – not just the colour, but the life, the expression and vitality that made her recognisable. She was like the animals I had found by the road, smaller than lifesize, already going to waste from the first moment she had stopped breathing. I brushed her hair and applied some perfume. I thought about make-up: a little lipstick, perhaps a touch of powder. Those things seemed appropriate, just as I knew she would look better for her best pearls and those classic, single drop pearl ear rings. I hesitated a long time before I could bring myself to remove her night-dress, but I knew it was needed for the ceremony. I wanted her to be naked on this, our last night together. In the morning, I would begin the normal business of doctors and funeral directors, but for now, in the silence of our locked house, I wanted to lie down beside her and sleep, under the white sheet, warming her with the blood-warmth of my living body, equals before death. After I had finished making her up, I applied the same thin film of lipstick and a dusting of powder to my own face, then I lay down beside her, my arms by my sides, my eyes closed. It was utterly still in the sickroom, but outside a bird called, and a gust of wind tumbled through the holly tree. For a long time I lay there, listening, waiting for the story to resume, or to reach some natural end. When I woke, it was morning, and I knew that I had dreamed, but whatever it was I had seen, I remembered nothing.

part two

lillian

For some weeks after the incident with Karen Olerud, I stayed at home, concentrating on my research. I could have worked at home all the time: it was quiet, I had everything I needed, and nobody ever came to the house. Sometimes I worked all night in the upstairs study. Sitting there, alone, surrounded by Mother's books, I felt a heightened awareness of everything around me; my skin was stretched tight as a drum; every sound reverberated in my spine; I registered every draught of air, every change in temperature. I could feel the deer moving in the woods, or drifting along the hedges; I heard dogs and foxes barking from miles away. At three in the morning, I would go out and stand in the garden. I would look up at the sky; I would taste the cool night air and I would feel as if I was the only person left in the whole universe, the one observer who was making it all happen. If anything, my visits to Karen Olerud had made me even more aware of my isolation in that house, but I had no desire to return. If I sometimes paused, in the middle of the day, remembering her wet flesh, I drove the image from my mind immediately. I no longer wished for the physical. I wanted to transcend the body. Occasionally, I would take the drugs Mother had left behind after she died; I would lie in her bed, half-conscious, drifting in and out of dreams, feeling my body dissolve, feeling my mind hover at the edge of another state, on the point of becoming something new.

It might have continued like this forever, if I hadn't decided to go back to the library at Weston one afternoon, while I was shopping. The library was small; most of the shelves were given over to popular fiction and accounts of true crime, with pockets of biography, gardening, home crafts, self-improvement, astrology, and the odd inexplicably wide selection of books on dog breeds or veteran cars. The reference section was set off to one side; it contained large format books and local histories, as well as a range of encyclopaedias and dictionaries. When I arrived, this section was empty. I took a book down from the shelves and opened it. I was struck by the quiet, and by the sense I had of having been there long ago – not déja-vu, but a thread of lost memory, a half-vision of a summer's day, long ago, when I was around twelve or thirteen. Suddenly I recalled sitting in this very room, working my way through the dictionaries, looking up the word for 'soul' or 'birth' or 'speech' in different languages, trying to understand the etymology, the underlying sense people had of the fact. I was certain, at the time, that language corresponded to the world, that essential truths were conveyed in the choice of a word: if a word existed, it existed for a reason; no matter how vague or unsatisfactory the definition might be, the very fact that a word for 'soul' was found in every language meant that something had to be present that corresponded to that word.

By then I had already begun experimenting with the living animals I caught in the woods, cutting them open and looking inside for that evanescent warmth or rhythm that might contain its essence. I had come to understand the beauty of anatomy: everything was finely structured, each animal was a wet machine made of tissue and filigree, a machine that could be taken apart and examined, down to the smallest component. I had not understood this before. The process of decay had rendered me passive, a mere observer, unable to intervene; but with the first dissection, I became a participant. I felt I had entered a secret domain, the domain that opened up beneath the scalpel and forceps. For a long time, I was happy. I felt it was possible that, by some effort of will, I would discover the truth.

Then, all of a sudden, everything changed. No matter what I did, there was something that slipped through my fingers, something that evaded the tip of the blade. I began to think of other possibilities, new horizons. I did not know where the soul resided, but suddenly I suspected that it was not in the body as such. Yet – if not there, then where? If not in flesh, or blood, or in the synapses of the brain, it had to be elsewhere. Perhaps it wasn't physical at all. Perhaps it was a process, like thought, or conversation. If the components of the body were organs and veins and cells, then the components of thought and language were words and grammar. It was just what Mother had been telling me all along: a creature without language is a creature without a soul. To know the soul, I would have to know language. It seemed so obvious, I was surprised not to have thought of it before. Now I had my true vocation. If I wanted to dissect the soul, I would have to use a new method, and develop different skills.

That sudden memory changed my life. I realised, in that moment, that my true vocation had begun there, in Weston Library, amidst the shelves of books on fish breeding and polar exploration. It was an entirely sentimental impulse that decided my fate, an unwarranted nostalgia, but this was the path that led to Lillian, and to the twins. I can say to myself that, if this had not happened, something else would, and it's true, but what matters is the course of destiny, the inherent order in things that drives us forward, so we make one choice rather than another and

each choice, no matter how trivial it seems, has the potential
to be decisive.

I began going to the library once a week. I would set myself
up in the reference room and make copious notes, searching
the shelves at random, looking for some connection that would
reveal the secret, knowing there could be no systematic way
to study this question, that any method or plan would impose
its own artificial logic on the very information I was finding.
I knew, if I had a specific idea, or a methodical approach
to the subject, I would miss some things and allow undue
weight to others, so I read almost indiscriminately, pulling
out encyclopaedia volumes, reference works, books on history
and mythology, making photocopies, spending whole days
deciphering obscure commentaries on the Old Testament or
sympathetic magic. When I found a reference to a text with
which I was unfamiliar I would ask Miss Patterson, the one
full-time librarian, to order it for me. Miss Patterson was my
immediate friend: a slight, middle-aged woman who looked
younger than her years, she always dressed immaculately, in
classic twin sets and simple strings of pearls or semi-precious
stones. Her hair was very black, but touched here and there with
a premature grey, and that, combined with her gold-rimmed
spectacles, gave her a studious, slightly quizzical appearance.
Sometimes she looked like a young grandmother, who had just
set aside her knitting to put away a few books; on other days,
it was as if she were a young woman disguised as an old lady,
concealing a firm, well-rounded body, a lithe energy, behind the
appearance of respectable womanhood. Generally, she treated
those who came in as visitors in what was essentially a private
space: she was courteous but distant, she answered questions
patiently, and with an impressive thoroughness, but her clients

were never allowed to feel entirely welcome. She treated every enquiry as casual. Nothing was to be taken too seriously.

With me, it was different from the beginning. I would sometimes become aware of her approving gaze as I sat in the reference section; she seemed to believe I was engaged in something important, that her library was now graced with the presence of a real scholar. Sometimes, when I was making an enquiry, or requesting an inter-library loan, she would ask how my work was going. Though I had never imparted to her the purpose of my research, and though she knew nothing more than the titles of the books I had ordered, she took an active interest. I think all she wanted was for me to tell her something, to take her into my confidence, to let her participate in some small way, but my answers were always non-committal, and I was careful to give no sign that her interest was welcomed. Still, my days at the library, and even these snippets of small talk, these moments of obvious admiration, made me feel I had a purpose, that I was getting somewhere. Sometimes, driving home, I would become aware of an odd feeling of pleasure, of satisfaction. Somehow, no matter how little I had actually learned, these hours of research made my work seem real, almost professional.

The drive to and from the library was the only outing I had all week. I would go in on the main road, but I would take the back way home, over the hill, where there was less traffic. In the evening, as the air darkened, I felt connected to the earth, as if the car were plugged into a current of oakroots and gas. My headlamps scanned the twilight, catching the shape of an owl in a thorn, or picking out the eyes of a fox on the road ahead, and I would feel included in something, in some ancient, pagan existence that had been disguised over the years, mopped up in corrupted place names, built over with chapels and supermarkets and wafer-thin housing estates. I sensed the joy and malevolence of this existence. I thought of it as multiple and hooded, a manifold spirit, like the *genii cucullatii* I had read about in a book on pagan Britain: those dark creatures of the verges and borderlines the Romans had adopted as companions to Mercury, the subtlest and least predictable of their gods, the unreliable carrier of messages. I wanted to know what they meant, those Hooded Ones. I wanted to understand how they worked, what gave them their power, what set them apart from other deities, so they were capable of anything, and seemingly immune to retribution or even judgement. If spirits existed, in any form, I thought, they would have to be like these: impersonal, neutral, rooted in the physical, utterly remote from human concerns.

The girl was sitting in the far corner of the reference section, with a pile of books — maybe twenty or more — spread around her on the table. At first I assumed she was a student, in her heavy knit sweater over a thin summer dress and her large, clumsy-looking work boots; her hair was long and wavy, and she was pretty in a pale-skinned, red-mouthed way, reminiscent of a thin child in poorly-applied make-up. But I could not help noticing, as time passed, that her approach was even less systematic than mine. She wasn't looking things up, or cross-referencing; she was simply turning the pages, gazing at the pictures, abandoning one book suddenly for another, quite unrelated volume, crouched over the table with her head down, her hair hanging over her face, or suddenly sitting up and looking around, as if she had just become aware of her surroundings. Once she caught me watching her and I turned away quickly. I could tell she was still watching me — I had a strong sense of her vague and aimless attention coming to focus upon me, and when I looked back at her she was still looking, quite unself-consciously, as if I were just another picture in one of her books. I turned away and pretended to work. When I glanced at her again, she had raised her knees so they rested on the edge of the table, and she was sitting back, sucking her forefinger, looking at a large-format book of black and white photographs. I could see she had no writing materials, no notebooks or sketch pads, like the other students who very occasionally visited the reading room. On closer observation I could see that her dress was a thin, billowy, almost see-through cotton, printed in blue and white with stylised cats or kittens, like something a child might wear. Her hair was clean, but her fingernails were dirty. She became aware of me watching her again, but this time she kept her eyes fixed on her book. It was as if she was letting me look at her, as if we were playing a game, making up the rules as we went along. From time to time she would flick through the pages of her book, then stop when she found a picture she liked. She would study it closely for a while, sometimes for ten minutes or more, then she would move on. There was no common theme in the choice of books that I could see. They were all large-format picture books, but the subject-matter varied – volumes on fashion, collections of photographs by Cartier-Bresson and Richard Avedon, monographs on the paintings of Stanley Spencer or Vermeer, a history of *Time-Life* magazine, books on birds, aviation, fishing, plantlife and travel, books of cartoons and recipes.

She was prettier than I had first imagined, almost beautiful, but there was something disconcerting about her. She could have been twenty, but she could as easily have been thirteen. While she allowed me to look at her, I had the idea that something was building silently between us, a kind of pleasurable tension, an expectancy, as if it would take only the slightest of signals for something to begin. There was something exciting about this, and dangerous too, like flirting with a child. For one long, dizzying moment I thought she was about to look up, to turn to me and speak. But nothing happened. Perhaps she was waiting for me to speak, perhaps I was imagining the whole thing, but that day, I had no opportunity to find out. I was still casting around, trying to think of something to say, when Miss Patterson appeared with a pile of books in her arms, and I quickly returned to my research – though not before she had caught my eye, and let me know, by her look, that she had read, or thought she had read, what was in my mind.

A few minutes later, a man appeared and stood across the table from the girl. When she looked up and saw him, her face was transformed to a white mask of fear and dismay. The man was dishevelled and unkempt, in black tennis shoes and a crumpled, powder-blue suit that must have come from a charity shop. His hands were thrust into his jacket pockets, as if to hide something, and he looked as if he hadn't washed or shaved in a couple of days. I could see Miss Patterson was gathering herself, waiting for something to happen that would give her an excuse to eject them both, but there was no need: as soon as she saw the man, the girl stood up, leaving her books spread out on the desk and, when he turned to leave, she followed, her arms hanging by her sides, her head bowed. I remember I was disappointed that she did not look back. Miss Patterson watched them out, then, as soon as the main door had closed behind them, came to my table.

'Dreadful people,' she said.

I nodded.

'I hope they didn't disturb you.'

'Not at all,' I answered. 'Who are they, anyway?'

'I don't know the man,' Miss Patterson replied. 'The girl's

been in a few times. I imagine she only comes here to keep warm.'

She shook her head.

'I don't think she can even read,' she continued. 'She just looks at the pictures. I asked her once if she wanted to join, but she didn't even answer.'

'Perhaps she's shy,' I ventured. I wanted to bring the conversation to an end, so I could leave, and perhaps find out where the girl had gone.

'No.' Miss Patterson looked determined. 'Did you see the way that man looked at her? I think she was hiding from him. That's why she was here. She wanted somewhere warm to go, where he wouldn't find her.'

I nodded vaguely and began gathering up my things.

'Are you leaving already?' Miss Patterson asked, almost in alarm.

'I'm afraid I must,' I answered. 'I have an appointment.'

She smiled tightly and nodded.

'We'll see you next week, then,' she said, and returned to her desk.

Outside, it was brighter than I had expected. I was sure the girl would be long gone, and I was kicking myself for having allowed Miss Patterson to detain me. Then, on the pavement, in front of Trinity Church, I saw them, the man and the girl and two other men, standing in a tight huddle, like a group of conspirators. The man from the library was talking and the other men were listening and nodding in agreement; they seemed to defer to him and I concluded that he was the leader of the group. Only the girl appeared to be paying no attention to what he was saying. The other men, who were both taller and slightly younger than the man from the library, were dressed in similar clothes and looked even dirtier and more unshaven than he did. After a few moments, they seemed to reach an agreement. One of the younger men handed a banknote over to the leader, with obvious reluctance. The older man pocketed the note, took the girl by the arm and led her across the road to the King's Head pub. The others tagged along behind them. I waited till they were inside, then I crossed the road and followed them into the bar.

The man who had come into the library was ordering drinks. Close to, he looked shorter: thin and wiry, around thirty-five, I thought, with a slight curve to his shoulders and long, greasy hair. His hands were grimy and chapped, but this did not disguise how small, or how oddly feminine they were, narrow across the palm, with delicate tapering fingers, and tiny, birdlike knuckles. The other men had taken seats at a table by the window, one on either side of the girl, who sat with her head bowed, her hair hanging over her face, her hands clasped in her lap.

When his drinks arrived, the man turned to me and raised his glass of lager. His voice was the most unpleasant I had ever heard: slightly high-pitched, calculatedly soft and insinuating.

'I don't know whether to drink this, or just look at it,' he said.

I nodded, but I did not speak. He smiled and shook his head slightly, then moved away, carrying three pint glasses between his hands, spilling a trail of drops across the wooden floor as he went. I noticed there was no drink for the girl.

I ordered a coffee and sat down at a table near the bar.

A moment later, the man was up again and walking towards me with a faint, fixed smile on his face. I thought he was going to speak again, perhaps even to ask for money, but he passed by and began feeding a handful of coins into the fruit machine, a few feet away. The man who had handed over the banknote got up and stood beside him watching, but the first man didn't seem to notice, he was so intent on the game. He seemed to be having some luck: with each stage of his success the machine sounded a peal of bells, then warbled out a fairground organ version of 'We're in the money'. Then, when a crisis loomed, it hurtled through the opening of the William Tell overture, and spat out handfuls of chunky gold tokens, which the older man scooped up greedily and fed back into the machine. His companion began to grow restless.

'Come on, Jimmy,' he said. 'You're going to lose it all again.'

Jimmy shook his head, but did not look up from the machine. He pressed a button several times with his hand, and William Tell sounded, followed by a deluge of tokens. He turned to his companion and grinned.

'The milky bars are on me,' he said, as he scooped up his winnings and made his way back to the bar.

I glanced across at the table by the window. The girl was still sitting with her head down, hands clasped, listening to something, some voice or sound only she could hear, far in the distance. The third man, who was younger and better-dressed than the other two, asked her if she wanted a drink, but she seemed not to hear. In all the time I had been in the pub, she had kept her head down, yet I was certain she knew I was there. Watching her, I imagined it was me she was listening for, as if my thoughts could travel across the lit space of the pub, and reach her without the others knowing – and for a moment, I thought she really could hear my thoughts, that she had listened in to me when we were in the library, and she was listening in now, as I sat watching her, only she was unable to acknowledge the fact, afraid of what her companions might do. Jimmy and his friend were still at the bar; Jimmy

91

was ordering lager and whisky, offering to buy the barman a drink, laughing and spilling coins on to the polished wooden counter. It might have been the noise of the tokens, spilling out of Jimmy's pockets, or perhaps it was something the young man beside her had said but, all of a sudden, the girl looked up and saw me, watching her across the room. I sat perfectly still and held her gaze. I was trying to tell her with my thoughts that she could leave these people and come with me – and I was sure she understood, because she smiled slightly, sadly, and shook her head almost imperceptibly.

I stood up. The third man had noticed me now, and he looked at the girl, puzzled.

'What is it?' he asked.

The girl resumed her former position immediately, with her head down, her hair hanging over her face. The third man looked at me suspiciously, then glanced towards the others at the bar. They had finished their order and Jimmy was standing, with a drink in one hand, watching him.

'What's up with you?' he asked and, before the third man could answer, I stood up, finished my coffee and went outside. I waited several minutes, to see if the girl had followed, but she did not appear, so I walked slowly back to my car, and drove home.

For the next several days I had the same dream, with minor variations, once, sometimes twice a night. I was walking in the evening, on a path through a leafy wood. It was that time of day when the light has softened – evening-time in late June, say. I half-recognised the wood: it was spacious and open, with tall beech trees and field maples on either side. Cow parsley grew thick and white along the path; the grass was long and flecked with cuckoo-spit; everything was still warm from the day's heat. There were blue shadows under the trees, but the light was mostly green – green with a suggestion of water, and traces here and there of that smell you can find in old bottles and cans. It was that time of the evening when you sometimes feel you are being watched, when something moves, a few feet away in the undergrowth, and you turn to almost see what must have been an animal, or a bird, vanishing amongst the leaves. I felt calm in the dream. I was walking slowly, enjoying the near-silence, the smell of the cow parsley, the cooling air. I felt calm and I had the sense of going to meet someone, keeping a long-planned appointment, somewhere further along the track. I think I had been walking for a long time when the dream began, content at first, then – quite suddenly – a little anxious, for no reason that I was aware of – anxious, or perhaps concerned, not unhappy, not afraid, nothing so extreme. After a time, I realised that what had disturbed me was the absence of birdsong, at that time of day when the birds should have been loudest, and I tried to remember whether I had heard them before, when I first set out. I thought I had, but I could not be sure; at the same time, the path widened and led me into a wide meadow. The grass had been cut here, it was dry and stubbled underfoot; at the far edge of the meadow I could see an old-fashioned wooden house, dark and vacant-looking, and in need of some repair, with a broken roof and a wide veranda at the front.

I began walking towards the house, convinced there was no one there, but curious to see inside. I was more aware of the quiet with each step I took till, as I stood at the foot of the veranda, the silence was total and oppressive. The windows at the front of the house were dusty and almost black, and a few were broken, giving on to a deeper blackness within. An old wheelbarrow stood in the yard. It had once been painted green, but now the paint was flaking away and the wood that showed was black and streaked with mildew.

I had been so sure that no one was there, it was some time before I noticed the man, sitting on a rickety wooden chair on the veranda. Even when I did see him, I thought at first that he was a model of some kind, a sculpture perhaps, or a shopfront dummy. My next thought was that he was dead, that he had died long ago, when the house was still intact, and he had sat there for years, waiting for me to find him. I concluded that he must have died of old age, because his skin was wrinkled and dark, and his grey hair and beard were long and matted, yet his clothes were clean, as if they had been newly laundered and replaced, some time recently. I wasn't afraid. I climbed the steps and stood on the veranda, looking at what I thought was his lifeless body. I noticed there was something familiar about the face, but I couldn't have said what it was. The eyes were closed, thin-lidded and wrinkled, like a bird's eyes, and his mouth was thin too, thin and small, smiling a little, I thought, as if he had thought of something funny and probably a little bitter, or sad perhaps, during his last moments. I could see that the teeth were brown with decay.

I was trying to think who he was, when his eyes opened, suddenly large and blue as robin's eggs, bright, alive, a little dangerous, and I stepped back, half-expecting him to reach out and grasp me with a long bony hand, like one of those monsters in Mother's fairy tales. He remained perfectly still. I understood then that he could not move his body at all, only his eyes. He was quite powerless.

It was this knowledge that decided my next move. As if I had known they were there all along, I took two small, bright-blue pebbles from my pocket and held them up to his face, so he could see. He seemed to be straining to keep his eyes open, as if even that small effort was too much for him, but he saw the stones, and he nodded, with what appeared to be a look of resignation. I reached out with my right hand, cradling the stones in my left, then plucked the right eye from his head and put it in my pocket. His body stiffened slightly; otherwise, he did not move. With the stones growing moist and warm in my left hand, I removed the other eye and placed it in my other pocket. The man's sockets were black now, and empty, like the old house behind him. There was no blood, and he remained still, as if he had felt no real pain. Then, slowly, and with great care, as if the whole world depended upon it, I took my pebbles, dropped them into his skull and watched as the eyelids closed and settled upon them. For a moment, I thought they were lost, that they were falling forever into that blackness; that the eyes would never be opened again, and I would have to stay there, with this blind old man forever – but, after a moment, the eyelids rose, slowly and with great difficulty. Now, the man did seem to be in pain; nevertheless, his eyes opened and now they were brighter and more blue than ever, joyful-seeming, empowered. There was no other change: his body remained in the rickety chair, his mouth was still thin and decayed, yet I could feel his happiness flooding me, just as I had felt his pain and dismay before. At the same time, I realised he was dismissing me, signalling with his new eyes that I was released from my obligation to him, that the spell that had held us both there was now broken. I took one last look at those brilliant eyes, then I turned, descended the steps of the veranda and began walking back across the meadow, the way I had come.

Each time I woke from this dream, I remembered the girl from the library, and I remembered how she looked at me that day, across the bar room of the King's Head. There was something about her that was important, I knew, but I couldn't work out what. All I knew was that I would find her again some day, because that was what was intended.

Several weeks passed before I saw the vagrants again. As the days hinted at autumn, I still visited the library, driving in across the hills, watching the woods as they turned gold and crimson. Miss Patterson continued to take an interest in my work; occasionally, that interest became intrusive. As a matter of fact, I think she had begun to develop an unhealthy interest in me. She would put aside whatever she was doing whenever I arrived and ask if there was anything I needed, anything special. I remained polite, but I made it clear that I wanted to be alone to concentrate on my work. Not that it made any difference. If anything, my remoteness only attracted her more.

One evening, as I was walking back to my car through Trinity churchyard, I saw the man Jimmy and the younger of his two friends, sitting on a bench at the far end of the garden, by the gate that led out to Cuthbert Street, where I would have to pass them, to get to the car park. It had rained earlier, and the bench must have been wet, but they didn't seem to care. They were sharing a bottle of cider, and smoking cigarettes; when they saw me, the young man stood up and lurched forwards with one hand outstretched.

'Spare us some change?' he asked, his voice a little slurred from the drink.

I shook my head and kept walking towards the gate. Jimmy was still seated, but he looked up at me as I approached and gave me a hard smile.

'Spare us some change, mister,' he said, quietly, insinuatingly.

I shook my head again.

'I know you, don't I?' he said more loudly, getting to his feet and peering into my face.

I stopped as he blocked my way.

'I don't think so,' I answered. 'Now, let me pass.'

It was a mistake, of course. He was looking for confrontation. Somewhere, at the deepest level of his being, there was an expectancy of contempt, a desire to be confirmed in the belief that the world was against him. He was looking for an opponent; he was looking for the first indication of repugnance or disgust, so he could strike back, and show his defiance. Not that I was concerned. I had carried small weapons and tools in my coat for years, for use in just such a situation. I had no intention of becoming a victim, especially the victim of vermin like these. That evening, I had a Stanley knife in my pocket, and I was ready to use it.

'No need to be like that,' he said.

The other man had turned back and stood behind me, watching, waiting for his cue.

'You could show people some respect,' Jimmy continued, and the other man echoed him, quietly, gloatingly. 'That's all I ask. It's not too much to ask, is it?'

I waited. There was no point in further conversation; if they were going to attack, they would do it now. I slipped my hand into my pocket and gripped the Stanley knife. There were two of them, but they were drunk and stupid, and I was alert. The knife would take them by surprise – people like Jimmy always assume superior strength, not because they are stronger, but because they think they are prepared to go further. It's the first law of human conflict: whoever is prepared to do the most damage, no matter what damage he suffers in return, will be the eventual victor. It's one of the qualities that distinguishes us from the animals, this readiness to throw caution to the wind. Faced with a real fight, most animals will compromise. If the odds look bad, one or another will back off, or the fight will be discontinued by mutual consent. Humans are the only animals prepared to fight for a Pyrrhic victory.

I had no reason to fight, of course. There was still a possibility of resolving the situation peacefully. Naturally, I had no desire to waste my energy brawling in a churchyard with two vagrants. If the men had attacked, I would have defended myself, and I have no doubt they would have come off worst. Had it not been for the girl, I would certainly have walked away from the situation – but as soon as I saw her, I realised that this was the moment I had been waiting for. Nothing happens by chance. Even if she didn't realise it, she arrived at that moment for a reason.

Now, all of a sudden she appeared. I hadn't seen her before, but she must have been there all the time, hidden amongst the bushes, watching. I didn't know if she was with them or if she had stumbled upon us by accident, as she emerged from her hiding-place. In spite of the weather, she was wearing her thin summer dress and plastic sandals. As if it had been scripted, her arrival diverted Jimmy's attention from me, and I used the moment's distraction to make my move. Before he could defend himself, I stepped forward and slashed the Stanley knife across his face, drawing blood.

Jimmy screamed out in pain and rage. I slashed at him again, making contact with his head, then I hit him hard, once, so he fell to his knees, clutching his face. I turned to face the other man, but he was backing away. As I had guessed from the first, he had no taste for a fight. He was only there because of Jimmy. I took two steps forward with the knife raised, and he turned and ran, leaving his friend at my mercy.

I looked at the girl. For the first time, I noticed that her face was badly bruised, and she had a bad cut above one eye, the kind of cut a boxer gets after a hard punch.

'Are you all right?'

She did not answer.

I was keeping an eye on Jimmy. He wanted to get up, but he couldn't. He was afraid. There must have been blood in his eyes, and I think the sight and feel of it deprived him of any will to fight on. I turned back to the girl. She was staring at Jimmy in horror and I realised she knew she would be blamed for this: as soon as I was gone, Jimmy would take it out on her. I was in no doubt that the bruises and cuts on her face were his handiwork. This would work in my favour, of course; it would help me persuade her to get away from there, if persuasion were needed.

I reached out and tried to take her arm, but she drew away. She had the look, now, of a hurt, frightened animal. Everything was a threat to her. She was as much afraid of me as she was of Jimmy. I didn't understand. Surely she remembered me. Surely she knew who I was and why I had come.

'Listen,' I said, 'I want to help you.'

She looked up. Her face was grimy and wet. Her dress was torn at the shoulder. She seemed not to have understood what I had said, or perhaps she had not heard and it struck me that she might be deaf.

'Can you hear what I'm saying?' I asked.

She did not answer, but after a moment she nodded.

'Can you tell me where you live?'

She shook her head. For the first time, she relaxed a little. I realised the questions were helping, there was something in the fact of my talking to her that made her want to trust me.

'Do you have anywhere to go?' I asked.

She shook her head again. Suddenly I realised, without knowing how I had reached the conclusion, but with utter certainty, that the girl was dumb, and my entire being was flooded with joy.

'Then come with me,' I said. 'I can help you.'

A flicker of hope crossed her face. I could see that she wanted to believe what I was saying, that she was desperate. Obviously, Jimmy had beaten her before. He probably did it on a regular basis, whenever he felt angry, or hurt, or bored. I imagine she knew as well as I did that, if she stayed there, he would give her the worst battering she had ever had, not because it was her fault, but because she had been present at his fall. There was every chance that he might kill her, for having witnessed his disgrace.

'Come on,' I said. 'You can get cleaned up and have a hot meal. Then you can decide what you want to do.'

I retracted the blade of the Stanley knife and put it back in my pocket. Jimmy was no longer a threat.

'Come on,' I repeated, 'or I'll have to leave you here.'

She hesitated a moment longer; maybe she half-understood that, by now, I had no intention of leaving her there, or of letting her decide anything. Maybe that was what decided her.

'You'll be safe,' I said.

She looked away, towards the far corner of the churchyard, where the other man had disappeared through the bushes. I think she believed he was still watching. Then she glanced back at Jimmy, still kneeling on the path, with his head bowed to the ground. I think she gave something up then, and cast her fate to the wind. Minutes later, she was sitting, her head bowed, her hair covering her face, in the passenger seat of my car, and I was driving her home, my heart racing with excitement at the thought of this strange new treasure that I would open and discover and explore.

Her name was Lillian. As far as I could tell, it was the one word she could write. She didn't stay with me for long, and I think of her now as a ghost who inhabited the house for a time, then slipped away silently, leaving me with the twins, as if she had been sent to me for that purpose alone. Perhaps she had. From the first, she was a complete mystery to me. There was no way of knowing what was in her mind. Most of the time, I suspect, she was vacant, or as vacant as it was possible for anyone to be and, even though I knew she could hear me when I spoke, I was convinced she had the power to switch everything off and sit there, a few feet away, completely alone inside her head, like the old foreign woman along the road, sitting in her cottage with the lights out, disconnected from the rest of the world. Sometimes I would call her by name and she would turn, surprised and uncertain, and perhaps even a little excited, as if she wasn't altogether sure that the word applied strictly to her. Then she would smile, pleased with herself, pleased with this small confirmation of her presence. It was hard to think of her as a distinct person at such times. She had the air of a newly adopted puppy, all attention, all eagerness to be seen; yet she was tactful, in her way, and she existed as lightly as she could, as if she was afraid she might outlive her welcome.

I never discovered anything of her history. She could hear, but she couldn't speak; she could read a little, I think, but she could not write. When I had won her trust, she scrawled her name on a large piece of paper, then drew a picture of herself alongside the word, to illustrate it. That was how her mind worked, I think. She saw pictures. She wrote slowly, with her left hand, twisting her arm, so her elbow pointed outwards. She looked even more like a child then but I don't think she was mentally deficient. It was as if she lived in a different space from the rest of the world. I soon forgot the idea that she could share my thoughts, or understand my intentions. Nevertheless, I would catch her looking at me, from time to time, and it seemed the mind behind that look was more penetrating, in its way, than the most incisive intelligence.

On the first night, I fixed the cut over her eye, got her cleaned up and put her in one of the guest rooms. She was so reluctant to assume a place, or take anything for granted, that I found her the next morning, asleep in her clothes on the kitchen floor, with her knees pulled up into her belly and her elbows folded in front, like the mummified princess I had once seen in a picture book. For three days she hardly moved out of the kitchen – the first place I had brought her to on that first night home. It was as if she imagined she belonged there, and had no title to the rest of the house. Whenever I was with her, she seemed to be watching me, waiting for me to leave her alone, and I thought she was afraid. She still wasn't sure I wouldn't harm her in some way. I didn't realise what she was up to till later, when I glanced out of an upstairs window, and saw that she was going out into the garden, when my back was turned, to urinate in the far corner, near the compost heap. After that, I made more of an effort to make her see that she was welcome. I introduced her, gradually, to the rest of the house: though I kept Mother's room locked, I let her know she was free to go anywhere she pleased, that she could touch and use things, that she could fill the kettle and make herself tea, and sit down at the table to drink.

Since she had nothing other than the clothes she stood up in, I decided that as soon as her bruises had healed, I would take her shopping in another town, far enough away to avoid recognition. She could have used Mother's things – she was almost the same height, though considerably thinner – but I didn't think it appropriate, at least to begin with. Besides, I wanted to make an occasion of the shopping trip, to win her trust and, if possible, find out something about her. I couldn't take the risk of our being seen together in Weston, of course, and I was sure, if I took her there, she would suspect me of wanting to return her to Jimmy. Naturally, I had no intention of doing any such thing. From the moment I had realised she was mute, a plan had been forming in my mind. It was perfect; it was elegant. However, first I would need to win her confidence, before I could set the plan in motion.

So it came about that, after a few days had passed, and she had begun to feel at home, I told her I was going to go out and buy her some more things to wear and, if she wanted, she could come too. I told her I wouldn't be going to Weston, but we would go somewhere farther away, where there were better shops, and if she wanted to, we could have lunch in a nice restaurant. We were sitting in the kitchen, having breakfast: she had a passion for toast, and ate it as often as she could, spreading the butter on thick, while the bread was still hot, then adding a layer of jam or marmalade and cutting the whole thing into longitudinal strips, before eating them, one by one, with obvious, even exaggerated relish. It was a ritual she performed, I think, for a kind of luck, as if a pleasurable moment in the morning would carry over into the rest of the day. As I described my plan, she kept working on her *confezione*. I tried to make the outing sound as attractive as I could; nevertheless, I still half-expected a guarded reaction. Instead, she was delighted.

I think that was one of the happiest days of her life. She seemed to like everything: the car journey, the shopping mall, the people. The smallest details excited and pleased her: cattle in a field, a children's play park, a boating lake. She pressed her face to the window and watched as the world flew by, like a speeded-up film. She stood gazing into shop windows as if she had just found heaven. It was amusing, how unself-conscious she was. Things pleased her, but she had no idea that they had to be paid for, that they were instruments of power. That morning we visited several good clothes shops. On arrival, the assistants would be amused at her appearance, and some played the snob card, looking down their noses at us, as we selected dresses and skirts and jumpers from the racks and Lillian tried them on, dancing out from the changing booth to show me, to receive my approval. In every case, I was the one who made the selections. I wanted to perpetuate that first impression she had made on me, that image of the gamine, half-child, half-woman. I suppose I found it erotic; yet it was appropriate too, the style expressed her very essence. I asked her, from time to time, what she liked, and when I chose something, I held it up for her to see, so I could observe her reaction, but she showed no preferences, no opposition to the image of her that I was creating. She was utterly innocent and, at the same time, she was intensely physical, stroking the fabric, smoothing it out over her thin body, holding out silk blouses or mohair sweaters so I could feel the textures. As each visit progressed, the assistants' amusement would change to puzzlement, then awkwardness, as the purchases mounted up, and it was obvious that this girl-woman was neither my daughter nor my wife. When it came time to pay, I paid in cash. I wanted to leave no evidence behind, nothing that could be traced to show we had been there. As the money changed hands, the well-dressed, well-groomed young ladies who invariably dealt with us would have to work at hiding their disapproval, while at the same time demonstrating, by an extreme and forced courtesy, that they had seen right through our little charade. Lillian noticed none of this. She was delighting in her day, delighting in herself.

When we had packed the car with bags and boxes, I took her to lunch. Once again, she made no attempt to conceal her excitement. It was as if she had never been in a restaurant before in her life. Perhaps she hadn't. Looking back, I realise that everything we did that day was new to her. When it came time to order, I chose avocado and prawns for her as a starter, followed by medallions of lamb with baby new potatoes and mixed vegetables. As soon as the bread arrived, she began spreading thick layers of butter on each slice; then, when the main course came, I had to order more butter, so she could drown her potatoes in thick yellow pats of running fat, and more bread, so she could wipe the plate clean of the lamb sauce. She ate everything, even the greens. People were watching us from the corner of their eyes: customers and waiters, giving one another sidelong embarrassed looks, as if we were performing some bizarre, slightly obscene ritual in their presence. For afters, I ordered a large, extravagant confection of ice cream and peaches for Lillian, while I sat quietly, drinking my coffee, watching her, and the whole room, with detached amusement.

But the finishing touch, the moment that sealed our complicity came as we made our way back to the car. We were passing a large store that sold electrical goods, computers and televisions and videos, row on row of large brightly coloured screens massed in the window so people could see there really was a world that went on without them, while they wandered the half-light of the mall, searching for whatever it was gave them comfort. Nothing is more wonderful than being able to buy what you want. Nothing is worse than seeing others buy in your place. A tall man in a baseball cap and bright purple trousers stood at the shop window, gazing hopelessly at the array of television screens, like someone standing at the gates of heaven, unable to find a way in. Lillian walked over and stood beside him. He glanced at her, then turned back to the twenty-odd images of Hedy Lamarr, in her Delilah costume, preparing to cut Samson's hair. Lillian was fascinated. She turned to me, to make me come and look – and I knew, in that moment that, while she wasn't asking for anything, she wanted a television more than anything else in the whole world. It was strange. Mother would never allow us to have a television set in the house, and I had honoured her wishes, even after her death, even though there were times I had thought it would be interesting to get programmes on nature and science and the news. Now, though I was fully aware of how much Mother would have disapproved, I took Lillian by the arm and led her into the shop, leaving the man in the baseball cap to his lonely vigil. As we found an assistant and I listened to him as he explained about screen sizes, and surround sound, and remote controls, and all the other marvellous features on offer, Lillian appeared genuinely confused. She seemed to find it difficult to imagine that we could just walk into a shop and buy a television set and, sensing this, I asked the salesman to throw in a good VCR as well. When the transaction had been completed, I told the assistant I would pick up the goods as soon as I had fetched my car. Then I turned to Lillian and told her the television was hers, just to see the look on her face. I thought Mother wouldn't mind, if she knew the full explanation for bringing those machines into the house.

That night, after we had gone to our separate beds, Lillian came to my door and stood watching me for some time. She was naked, a thin waif with her thumb in her mouth, gazing through the half-dark till I sat up quietly and drew back the covers. She did not hesitate for a moment. As she slipped in beside me, I understood that this was the one gift she had to offer in exchange for what she must have perceived as a near-imperial generosity. When I held her, she felt thin and fragile, and I have to confess that I didn't know quite what to do with her, that it was she who guided me, and drew me into the wetness of her childlike body. I still had no idea of how old she was and, though it was obvious she knew what she was doing, the idea that I was having sex with a child was pleasurable and exciting. I had not expected to feel so intensely, to want her so much, to be overwhelmed, almost, by my desire. In every human transaction, the first and decisive question is: who is in control? This is so commonly understood, it has become a cliché – but its truth remains unaltered, no matter how many people recognise it. Of course, control can be established in any number of ways, but it is important not to lose it, and it is not always the stronger who governs. The weak have many and varied stratagems, some unconscious, some planned. For a moment, the transaction I had entered into with Lillian hung in the balance: I could so easily have fallen under the spell of her thin body, her deliberate sensuality, her profound innocence. What I remember most clearly now about that night is the exultation of taking her roughly, for the second time, and of causing her to flinch, and to hold me closer in her pain, knowing she would be mine to do with as I wished, that it was her choice, not mine, that had made her my possession.

So a regime of sorts was established. It gave her pleasure to keep house, to tidy the rooms, to make simple meals, to carry out the rubbish and wash the dishes. It was a highly domestic life. She wanted to look after me, I think. She wanted me to be happy. For my part, I still desired her with the same intensity I had experienced on that first night. I couldn't keep my hands off her. I would find her in the kitchen and lean her over the table, or I would catch her halfway up the stairs and have her there, lifting the hem of the skirt or the dress I had bought for her and slipping off her plain white cotton panties, so I could enter, while she clung to me, making low gasping sounds and moving back and forth, gripping me tightly with her legs. I knew her response could be put down to gratitude, at least to some extent, for the things I had given her, but I believe she was genuinely fond of me, after her fashion. She had never expected such a life, and she couldn't help but like the one who provided it. Meanwhile, I would go out from time to time and bring home presents, baubles and toys that she would accept with the same delight, the same gratitude, no matter how expensive or how insignificant the gift might be.

In the early evenings, we watched television. I had set it up in her bedroom and we would watch it together. Lillian chose the programmes we watched. We liked American shows, especially the ones where people were spontaneous and natural in a quite unsentimental way, the shows that are broadcast between four and seven in the evening, half-hour situation comedies that centre on clean-living families with clever children in neat, middle-class suburbs. I think this was Lillian's idea of heaven: a boy cycling along a wide empty street in the early morning, tossing newspapers on to front porches; old men sitting on a veranda at dusk in Saratoga Springs or Boise, Idaho; women making pies in wide kitchens, surrounded by dogs and precocious children. It was the houses we enjoyed, as much as the people; each room was a character in its own right. We loved them for the space and the impossible light, the suggestion of woods, just a short walk away, deer in the shadows, coyotes in the hills.

These houses always contained at least three children. They were wise, and sometimes too clever for their own good; they were always learning small lessons; they always had the best lines. I liked it when they did things together, *en famille*, things they had evidently rehearsed and perfected over years, little routines, dance steps and songs, sequences of strange, ritualised movements which suggested an infinite self-regard, a bottomless appetite for appreciation. That was their strength, of course: they were appreciators. They appreciated themselves and they were learning to appreciate other people. The routines were there to say to the audience: look at us, look how easy it is to be honest and free and spontaneous, to take nothing less than the best, to meet the world on your own terms. Even when the hard lesson had to be learned, or some tricky situation had to be resolved, they were always ready: the twelve-year-old in the stripy shirt and baseball cap, the girl with freckles and a winning grin, the boy who had tried to duck responsibility – they would gather themselves up to say what had to be said, to do the right thing, to sacrifice their own wishes to the greater good. This was what democracy meant. Lillian and I would sit watching in silence, with involuntary smiles on our faces, happy for a while that the world could seem so right, the way it was supposed to do at Christmas or during childhood holidays, when everybody worked together and tried really hard.

Strangely enough, though, Lillian's favourite programme was the news. She would cry when she saw children starving in Africa, or bodies lining the streets of shanty towns in South America, but she never missed a single broadcast. She seemed gifted with an infinite capacity for sympathy: she felt for others at random, from the baby with the hole in her heart to the hundreds or thousands killed in the latest natural disaster. Most of all, she was a sucker for the human interest story. One evening, we watched an American hostage being released. For a time it looked as if nothing would happen: the cameras were all bunched together, filming each other in what looked like a hotel conference room, perhaps recently and hastily reclaimed from a convention of self-improvement junkies, or air-conditioning salesmen. Suddenly, the man appeared: a tall, bearded, suitably gaunt figure, surrounded by uniformed men, looking uncomfortable and out of place in his plaid shirt and trainers. He was blinded for a moment by the cameras, but he kept gazing out into the crowd, as if he expected to see a familiar face – a friend, or a wife, or a daughter. He had probably been briefed about what to expect, but I imagine something else had taken over as he walked free, a basic need to mark the moment, to celebrate or ritualise it somehow. Then he sat down and began to answer questions. What he said meant nothing; it was just that speech was the one celebration that remained to him, the pleasure of speaking and being heard, of speaking his own language and having people pay attention, instead of spitting on him, or striking him in the face with a rifle butt. That was what caught my attention every time: not so much the elation of the freed man, or the anguish of the victims, or the joy and guilt of those who had survived, but the fact that it always happened in public, amongst strangers, amongst people who were only doing their jobs, reporters and soldiers and cameramen, or the merely curious, who have drifted into the frame, distracted for the moment from their own lives. I was always amazed at how easily they talked about what had happened to them, the hostages, the victims, the survivors. I was always amazed by their need to speak, and by the way they adapted their speech to suit what was demanded – the snappy phrase, the truism, the cliché.

The hostage had been a captive for three years. Most of that time, he had been held in a small room, with no natural light; sometimes he had been forced to wear a hood, sometimes he had been beaten; no one had spoken to him for the first eighteen months, and he had been forbidden to speak. If he asked questions he was beaten. He had never seen the faces of his captors, they had worn masks or hoods when they brought his food. Sometimes that had heartened him: it allowed him to think they were afraid he would be able to identify them some day, when he was freed. But then again, he thought, the masks might be there for another reason entirely. Perhaps they were a means of distancing the terrorists from their prisoner, to avoid any human contact so that, when the time came to shoot him, they could do so without compunction. The hostage hadn't known he was to be released until his captors left him at the corner of one bombed out street and another, a few days before the press conference.

As I watched, I wondered what he had thought about during the three years of his captivity. At first, I imagine, he had missed his family, his own house, his bath, his kitchen, his bed. Then, perhaps, he thought back on his home town, his first lover, days he had enjoyed, moments that shamed him. I imagined him examining his life, letting it run in his head like an old movie, a movie he had seen once before but hadn't watched with such close attention to detail. Perhaps there were moments, during those weeks of self-examination, when he felt liberated, able to make peace finally with his dead, or understand the motives of those who had hurt him years before, for no reason. Surely he would have learned something about himself during those weeks. Yet, just as surely, he would have moved on to something less coherent, a disjointed sequence of vague memories and half-thoughts, and I wondered if, by the end, he had elected to be changed by his experience, or whether he had come back determined to have his old life back, just as it was. What had he missed? What had he promised himself in the dark hours when he knew for sure that he was going to be killed? What had he promised in the moments of hope, when he believed he would be released? I wanted to know. I imagined myself in his position, thinking of the pleasures to come: the smell of new books, the taste of coffee, snow on a pine tree, birdsong. These were the pleasures I imagined for him, but his imagined pleasures would have been different and, for that moment, I wanted more than anything to know what they were. Most of all, I wanted to know how he had talked to himself in his captivity, what he had said, and how he had said it, what linguistic choices he had made. I wanted to know if he had ever suspected himself of deliberately creating a lie, the myth of an ordered life, using words and silences to make things tidy and neat and clean. Surely, that would have been inevitable. Under such circumstances, an ordered illusion is necessarily preferable to the chaotic truth of the world.

I glanced at Lillian. She was gazing at the close up of the man's face with an awed expression, but for once, she wasn't in tears. She looked happy. She looked inextinguishably happy.

It was winter. The house was sealed away again, behind a veil of snow, invisible from the village. Lillian and I grew closer, and as the relationship developed, I felt closer to everything else too, more in tune with the world. There were places in the house I had never really understood: the airing cupboard, the shelves under the sink where Mother had stored shoe-black and oven cleaner. One afternoon, when the sun emerged, Lillian took the laundry out and left it there all night, so our clothes froze solid, and seemed to take on a life of their own. It was a long time before they thawed, standing in the kitchen sink, or dripping icy water on the floor of the scullery. All that night, it was as if the house was peopled with the ghosts of ourselves, the shapes we would make, if we were to step out into the cold and walk away.

Nobody knew Lillian was with me. My visits to the library at Weston had ceased and, though I am sure Miss Patterson wondered where I was, I am equally certain that she would not have suspected anything out of the ordinary. Now, instead of spending one day a week at the library, I would go shopping, wandering for hours through the supermarket aisles, where I had once sailed by, picking up convenience foods and basics. Now, with Lillian in the house, I paid more attention to this weekly ritual. Suddenly, I was tempted by new products, by the scent of fresh fruits, the crackle of packaging, the compact feel of things when they are cling-wrapped or packed tightly into fours and sixes. I bought oranges in net bags, exotic yoghurts, tropical fruits, boxes of dates, round-shouldered jars of cherry jam and acacia honey. I bought every variety of peanut butter. I bought Turkish Delight, asparagus spears and crystallised ginger. I bought foods I thought Lillian would like, the kinds of food you might buy for children, sweet things, buttery things, things dipped in chocolate or Marmite. I looked for things she might never have tasted: pawpaws, partridge, dressed crab. Most of all, I bought things for their names, for the wording on the packets, for the promise of health or self-indulgence they suggested – the more transparent the ploy, the more readily I seized upon it.

In the same vein, I bought her soaps and talcum powders, perfumes in atomiser bottles, fruit or herb-flavoured shampoos, because I liked the names, or the pictures on the bottles, or the tasteful design of the labels. I would spend a long time comparing, pondering, declining, returning, giving in. I was fascinated by soaps: they came in such infinite variety – the unassuming, the blatantly overpriced, the pure and simple, the transparent, the medicated, the exotic. Cucumber. Aloe vera. Elancyl. Wheatgerm.

No doubt anyone watching would have been amused – but

there is a safety in supermarkets, a feeling that, no matter what you do, you won't be held accountable when you leave the store, as long as you pay your bill on the way. People would go there for days out, amazed at the range of things you could buy. Each week, a new line appeared: children's clothes, videos, romantic books, alcoholic lemonade. One afternoon, I watched an elderly man work his way through a display of collectors' postage stamps, trying to decide what to buy. The packs were arranged by theme and by country, or they came in mixed batches of fifty or a hundred. Systematically, the old man removed each pack from the rod, lifted it up very close to his face, raised his glasses and peered underneath at the contents. Then he set that pack down on the floor, so he could get to the next. Finally, when he had worked his way through the entire display, he replaced each pack in order, and walked away. Later I saw him picking through the children's books. It seemed to me that he was one of the dispossessed, someone who only wanted to be close to goods, to touch them, to imagine their purchase, in order to feel complete. He was carrying a basket: it is always a sign of real or virtual poverty, to be carrying a basket, rather than pushing a large, well-laden trolley. He was a thin, round-shouldered man; his shoulders were flecked with dandruff and when I moved closer, to see what book he was about to choose, I noticed the smell of stale sweat and greasy hair. He became aware of me then and turned. I looked away, but it was too late: taking up his basket the man stalked off, offended and shamed. I felt as if I had deprived him of some basic right, a vital human dignity, a sense of himself as viable in a world of slogans and catchphrases, and words that meant nothing, but expressed the most precious of our dreams and aspirations.

When I returned, I found Lillian in bed. She seemed worried

and unhappy, and all my gifts for her made no difference. At first I thought she was ill. She looked pale, and she had been off her food for a couple of days. I asked her if she wanted a cup of tea, and she nodded, so I started for the kitchen, wondering what I could do to make her feel better. I was halfway down the stairs before I realised what was happening. I rushed back upstairs and tumbled into the bedroom. I was sure that my intuition was correct. Now I knew why she had looked so worried.

'It's all right,' I said.

She sat up in bed, gazing at me, like a pet that feels it has done something wrong, and is waiting to be punished.

'It's all right,' I repeated. 'Really. I don't mind. Not at all.'

She seemed unsure for a moment, perhaps wondering if I really had understood. I nodded happily, and then she saw that I knew, and she smiled.

I walked over to the bed and laid my hands on her shoulders.

'It's going to be fine,' I said. 'You'll see. Everything's going to be fine.'

I really believed that. I really did think it was true. I had no reason to worry, after all. Lillian had no family, as far as I knew, and as for Jimmy – well, I assumed he would just disappear. It was obvious, from his behaviour in the churchyard, that he was basically a coward, the kind of man who feels powerful if he has a woman to beat, or weak friends to follow him, like the men I had seen in the pub. I had encountered his kind before, men who slept rough in the churchyard or the park, and sat there all day, drinking cider, crouched amongst the headstones or sprawled out on the grass, men who fought in the filthy corners of the town, flailing at one another drunkenly, urinating behind the church – these men were virtually sub-human, and almost incapable of meaningful thought. They spoke, of course, but their speech was nothing more than a stream of sound, a barrage of noise and curses, as insignificant as the trails of urine they left against the churchyard walls. Their lives were meaningless, and they knew it. Their only power lay in the fact that they had nothing to lose. Nothing had any value for them.

For quite a while, there was no sign that Jimmy had traced Lillian to me. Then, one morning, after an early snow, I stepped into the garden, to take out the rubbish. It was a bright, cold morning. The snow was beginning to crust and turn to ice, but I could see that someone had walked the length of the path, from the front gate to the corner of the house, leaving a trail of dark, hard footprints. He must have come in the night or the early morning, when the snow was still fresh; now the tracks were old, beginning to fade into the ice. They were surprisingly small, barely a man's prints at all, more like the tracks left behind by an animal – but then, I remembered Jimmy's hands, how small they were, how delicate. I was sure he had been my visitor and I wondered what he had seen, or if he had taken anything. More importantly, I was alarmed that he had found us: if he could trace us to the house, then others might. I could only imagine the problems, and the danger to the future of the experiment, if the so-called authorities found a pregnant Lillian under my roof.

If that had been an isolated incident, I would have put it out of my mind. Further action was, as yet, unnecessary. There was no sure proof that it was Jimmy, after all. Though I had jumped to the conclusion that the tracks were his, I reminded myself that my nocturnal visitor might have been any vagrant looking for a place to sleep or something to steal. I checked the house for signs of forced entry; I checked the shed to see if he had found his way in there. Nothing was missing, there was no hint of attempted

116

burglary, and I managed to put the incident out of my head. It was coming up to Christmas, and I was thinking of what I would buy for Lillian. I wanted to make the occasion special. I had even considered giving her some of Mother's jewellery, or some perfume, but that seemed too much like sacrilege – better to go into Weston for something. If nothing else, I could use the visit to see if Jimmy was still there, or whether my suspicions were unfounded. I decided to drive over that morning.

Lillian was still asleep. She looked strange, lying in my bed, like a thin animal, with one hand raised to her mouth, as if she wanted to suck her thumb, and was only just managing to prevent herself. I watched her for a while: there is a real pleasure in watching another person sleep, listening to their breathing, wondering what they are dreaming, and what happens between the dreams, in the long dark gaps when absence takes over. I would have given so much to enter her mind, just for an hour, while she was sleeping. I think I would have preferred seeing her dreams to seeing her thoughts. I sensed a potential there, a possibility of real light and movement, a vividness which her thinking probably lacked. In many ways, in fact, I suspected Lillian of not being a thinking creature at all: she gazed at pictures, she watched television, she cried when a programme was sad, she smiled at a sentimental or conventionally beautiful image, but there was little evidence of a thinking response. Not that I liked her the less for that. There were times when she was almost beautiful, lying asleep, or staring into space, and I believe the effect was heightened by her simplicity. There were times, I know, when I felt a genuine affection for her and now, more than ever, she was precious to me, for the part she was about to play in my life's work.

I spent the morning in Weston, trailing from one shop to another, buying odd gifts, for Lillian and for myself. I wished

I could have taken her with me, so she could pick what she wanted, or so I could watch her try on the dress I would give her later, when I reached home. I wanted to know if she was ready to make her own choices, or whether she would still rely on me to pick things out for her. I wanted to buy her maternity clothes, and things for the baby.

It was a bright, snowlit day, warm in the sun, icy in the shadows. I took the path through Trinity churchyard: there was no sign of Jimmy or his friends. I stopped a while and walked between the headstones, brushing packed ice from the holly shrubs and watching it fall. I remembered how glad I was, as a child, when winter came, when the air was crisp and the puddles froze along our lane. I felt just as I had then, and I realised I was happier than I had ever been since Mother died. My body felt solid and real, like something made of glass or metal. I felt having Lillian in the house had something to do with that sensation of well-being, of total physical integrity, and I wanted to buy her something special.

There is such a simple and clean pleasure in shopping for inessentials: you decide what you want, from amongst marvellous hordes of possible alternatives, then you pay for it. Nothing is out of reach, nothing exists that cannot be possessed. Then, when the purchase is complete, the object feels strange, exotic, almost uncalled for. It's such an innocent and perfect pleasure, this moment of possession. Some objects are more pleasing than others – things made of glass, for example, things made of silk, or polished wood, whatever is metallic or mineral, anything that relates to water. Best of all are the old-fashioned butchers, or fishmongers, where you can buy whole rabbits or pheasants, or carry home a heavy, bright salmon, fresh from the sea, the light still glittering in its eyes. Or pet shops, with their glass cases full of angelfish or darts; their warm, dark cages, packed tight with the stink of guinea pigs; their blue-green terraria, where snakes and lizards try desperately to blend in with the decor.

I didn't notice anything out of the ordinary till I was making my way back to the car. I had returned through the churchyard: once again, there was no sign of the vagrants amidst the darkening shrubs, or on the bench by the far gate. I might not have noticed anything at all, if I hadn't caught sight of a flicker in the hedge, just as I reached the car park. When I looked back, I saw it was only a blackbird, but immediately, I was aware of someone watching. I couldn't tell where it was coming from; it was a general sensation, like the feeling you have as a child, when the teacher in school tells you God is watching. There was no evidence of anyone being there: the grounds were still, and silent. Yet I was certain I was being observed by someone, or something. I stood still, and waited. The sensation lasted no more than a few seconds, maybe half a minute; then the blackbird flew noisily from out of a shrub, a shower of snowflakes flickered from the hedge where it disappeared, and the feeling passed. A moment later, I was telling myself that the whole thing had been an illusion, a trick of the air. Yet still I felt uneasy, and I didn't relax altogether until I had reached the exit road, where the new snow shone on the hedges and the fields looked empty and wide, like fields in a Dutch landscape, where nothing will ever move or change again.

Someone had been there while I was gone. A trail of fresh-looking tracks led from the lane to the front of the garage. When I got out of the car to open up, I found a small pool of viscous greenish liquid by the door, as if someone had maybe tried to pour oil, or some other substance, into the lock. I tried the door. It was still secure, and undamaged. I looked back along the lane – uselessly, of course, since whoever had done this was long gone. I had passed nobody on the road, but whoever it was could easily have made his way through the woods, or across the fields. Obviously, Jimmy had found out where I lived; he must have guessed Lillian was still there – perhaps he had even seen her through the windows. Who knew how long he had been watching us, formulating whatever plan he had for his revenge? And how soon before he moved? I could not rely on his cowardice forever and the thought passed through my mind that perhaps he had enlisted someone else, one of his friends from the pub, to help him. That would have explained my feeling of being watched in the churchyard. If anyone had been there, he couldn't have been the person who had tried to break the lock of the garage, not unless he had a car, or some other means of transport. I was pretty certain Jimmy didn't have a car, which meant, logically, that he had an accomplice. I decided that I must confront him, as quickly as possible. It had to end. Now, for the first time, I had something to lose, and I was determined to defend it, at any cost.

I drove to Weston several more times before I found him. For a while, I thought he really had left, that I had imagined the whole thing, or misinterpreted signs that were, after all, more than a little ambiguous. I decided, if I didn't find him, that I would give up my search after a week, and wait to see what happened next. Even if I wasn't mistaken, he might have had no more in mind than making his presence felt, by these trivial and childish practical jokes. Not that I was prepared to tolerate that for any length of time. I wasn't prepared to take any risks.

As it happened, I encountered him on the fourth day, on my way back to the car. It was evening, and the churchyard was deserted. As soon as I saw him, I decided the only solution was immediate and decisive action. People like Jimmy are unpredictable: a little too much to drink, an argument with one of his cronies, and he might decide to take things further. I wasn't about to let my plans be jeopardised by a vagrant.

He was sitting in his usual place, on the bench at the far end of the churchyard, next to the gate. He was dressed in what looked like new clothes – a clean white shirt and jeans, a nylon jacket, a pair of brown leather shoes. He was newly-washed and clean-shaven, his hair combed to one side, with a pronounced centre parting. It made him look like a schoolboy. He saw me coming, but he made no attempt to get away. There was a bottle of cider on the seat beside him, and a plastic bag at his feet that looked like it might contain another bottle. He seemed drunk. Perhaps that had made him confident. He looked at me with feigned calm, and tried to seem unafraid. He seemed to be alone.

'You're still here,' I said.

'It's a free country,' he replied, bitterly.

'I thought you'd have moved on somewhere,' I persisted.

'I'm waiting for somebody,' he said.

'Who?' I asked.

'A friend.' He was trying to sound laconic.

'Your accomplice?'

He looked up, in surprise, then he turned away. He seemed not to understand what I meant, yet his manner disturbed me. After the first few seconds, he seemed more resigned than confident, as if he had determined to see things through, no matter what. There was no obvious threat in his voice, but the look in his eyes was unmistakable. It was the look of a man who had the taste of real power, perhaps for the first time in his life – not the power that came from bullying a confused girl, or one of his half-crazed companions, but the power that comes of knowing, of seeing through another man, and deciding to find him inferior. He had erased all doubt from his mind: he was certain he had caught a glimpse of my soul in all its ugliness, and the pleasure of knowing that I was just as bad as him was something he was trying hard to contain. He wanted it to last. He would go to any lengths to keep this shred of power; he had no way of knowing that whatever he had guessed about me was wrong. For my part, I was intrigued to know what he imagined I had done with Lillian. I was already sure that he knew I had her.

'How can you be sure your friend will come?' I asked.

'She'll come,' he answered quietly. 'She always does.'

I nodded. He was talking about Lillian, not an accomplice, and I think he really believed she would come back to him.

'Have you been waiting long?'

'A while. Not long.'

'It doesn't look like she's coming. Maybe she's left you.'

'I don't think so.'

I smiled.

'I know so.'

He looked at me with contempt. I was surprised – it seemed genuine.

'She'll be back,' he said.

I was touched. I could tell how much it mattered to him, how much he needed her. He needed his power over her, that power of knowing there was someone in the world that he could control. It filled a gap in the very fabric of his being. He had grown so used to it, it was a piece of himself, the spine of his identity.

'Not this time,' I answered softly.

'Then something's happened to her.' He looked up at me accusingly. 'I'll have the police on you.'

I laughed.

'Why would the police listen to you?' I said.

He shook his head. For a moment I thought he was going to cry.

'Maybe you have her now,' he said, at last. 'But she'll come back soon enough. All she wants from you is your money.'

I let him see that I was feeling sorry for him. There is no triumph quite like pity. The brave face he had been putting on had just crumbled before my eyes, and he felt it. A wave of helpless anger swept through him and he stood up.

'You don't know her,' he said. He gestured towards the bushes by the fence. 'I used to take her in there. I used to share her with my friends. You know? We used to go in there and fuck her senseless.'

He waved me away in sudden, desperate defiance.

'I know you. You're all the same,' he said. 'I know all about you. Don't think I don't know what you're up to. I'll have the police on you, you understand?'

He lurched away, forgetting his bottle, and made for the gate. I went after him. Even then, I think, I only wanted to finish the business I had come to settle, to frighten him off so he would stop coming to the house. If I had planned what happened next, I might never have gone through with it. I would have considered the risks. I would have weighed up the pros and cons, and I would probably have decided against it. In truth, I believe he brought the whole thing on himself. There was something in the way he backed away that only provoked me to follow.

By the time I caught up, he was standing at the top of the back steps to the church. I reached towards him, trying to make him stop, but I must have stumbled and pushed him, so that he fell backwards, teetering and flailing as he crashed heavily to the ground, taken completely by surprise. There was an expression

123

on his face – a kind of sadness, as if he felt deceived, as if there had been an agreement between us that I had wilfully broken. Maybe it was that look that decided me, maybe it was just a special form of logic that made me kick him as he tried to get up, then kick again, first in the face and head and then, repeatedly, in the back and stomach. I have no memory of how many times I struck, all I remember is the exaltation that surged through my body as my feet hit home, finding the cheekbones, the ribs, the soft plates of his groin. It was as if something had unfurled along my spine, a wave of power, unwinding in my body like a spring. He twisted away; he even tried to defend himself at first, but after a while I was free to aim my blows, smashing into the jaw and the teeth, finding the bridge of the nose, bursting the lips and the soft meat around the eyes, pummelling at the spine till I felt something shift and founder. He stopped moving – or rather, he only moved when I kicked him, turning with the blows like a bundle of rags. It was surprising how quickly the substance leaked out of him. By that time, some of the excitement had ebbed, but I kept going – calm now, systematic in a way I would never have imagined possible. It was as if this was something I had always wanted to do, as if I had never understood the reality of flesh and bone till that moment. I had imagined it structured and tidy, like the bodies in those illustrations by Vesalius, but this was nothing like that. Now, with a series of well-directed kicks, something snapped or shattered and the body at my feet changed into something new, more chaotic, less divinely-ordered. The calm I had attained by then was cold and clinical: it was fascinating to watch his body turn into meat. His eyes and mouth were unrecognisable blurs; oddly, one ear appeared to be partly-severed, and his head lolled to one side, like the head of a broken doll. At the same time, he seemed so relaxed.

I was tired. Now that the first rush of adrenaline had ended, I could feel the energy bleeding away. I stopped kicking. I knew Jimmy was still alive – I could hear him breathing, a thick, gurgling sound as if the blood had run into his mouth and throat. I looked around. There was no one in sight, yet I felt I was being watched, all of a sudden. It was quite dark by then. The lamp in the alley had come on, a pale orange that made the blood seem dark and flat around the fallen man. I looked down. My clothes were spattered with blood, but in that light it might have been oil, or dirt. Nobody seeing me would have known what had happened. A second wave of energy ran through me – a slow warmth, not a rush like before, but a wave, a gradual movement that filled my whole body. I was aware of a profound pleasure, but it was not altogether mine, it was abstract somehow, as if it came from everything around me, from the shrubs and the light and the dark blue of the sky. The world was so massive, so mysterious. I remembered a game I had played with myself as a child. Standing like this, under an orange streetlamp, I would look at my clothes and wonder what colour they really were – were they grey and blue, as they seemed in the daylight, or were they really, for that moment at least, this other colour they appeared to be under the light? The absurdity of this memory struck me immediately, and I almost laughed out loud.

I looked at Jimmy. He seemed small and empty, and I felt sorry for him again. He had never really understood anything that had happened to him. Even he had probably seen that his need for Lillian was pitiful, the craven attachment of a desperate man to whatever drifts his way. He had been on shifting ground all his life. Everything he had ever said was bravado.

I bent over the body and peered into Jimmy's face. It was cold now, and I was pretty certain he would die if I left him there, in his light clothes. On the other hand, someone might find him. The only logical thing to do was to finish him off; there was no other choice. If he was found, and managed to report what had happened, he might put the experiment in jeopardy. I reached into my pocket for a weapon and found it empty. The Stanley knife must have fallen out somewhere, yet I was sure it had been there when I left the house.

I looked around. I was not quite sure what I wanted – a stick, a piece of rope – I wasn't thinking straight. My eyes lit on the plastic bag under the bench. It was still there, where he had left it; when I looked inside, I found what I instantly understood was the answer to my problem and I was strangely grateful, as if he had provided the solution deliberately. The bag contained a full bottle of supermarket whisky – not the cider I had imagined – a packet of cigarettes and a box of Swan matches. Everything I needed was there. I dragged Jimmy into the shadow of the bushes near the fence, then poured the whisky over his face and chest. I emptied the whole bottle, making sure as much as possible coated his face and shirt, then I struck a match and tossed it on to the body. It caught fire with a sudden rush, a bluish flame that turned to red immediately. Jimmy moved, as if he wanted to stand up, but it only lasted a moment, before he fell back, wrapped in a sheath of fire.

I backed away. I was surprised by the heat, and how easily he had caught fire. The shirt was burning, it was some kind of synthetic, and that was what I smelled at first. Then, within moments, something else broke through – a sickening aroma of burning skin and hair, nothing like what I would have imagined. The face blistered and seared in the flames, the hair fizzled away, and I knew, before I left him, that there was no way he could have survived.

It was finished. It was a little unpleasant, at the end, when he was burning, but I soon put it behind me and walked away as casually as I could. The thought that someone was watching from somewhere occurred to me again, but instead of bothering me, it made me feel even more detached, as if what I had done was sanctioned by that invisible witness. I remembered a story Mother had told me, about an Antarctic expedition – how the men had imagined that someone was walking alongside them, but when they turned to look at him, he disappeared. The explorers had said that this phenomenon had never made them uneasy; they had even felt comforted by it, when they ran into difficulties. That was how my secret accomplice felt to me – an elusive companion whose presence was eerie but, at the same time, oddly reassuring.

It was that beautiful time of night when the air is fresh and the stars begin to show in the dome of the sky. The houses on Cuthbert Street were lit. I had an image of the people inside, sitting down to supper in their warm rooms, made quiet by the time of day and the season. I imagined them behind their curtains, diffident with one another, careful of things, aware of their own precious transience. I knew they were there, but I still felt alone in the world; it was as if they existed in a parallel space, like my unseen companion. I might have been invisible at that moment, running my hands through a wet hedge to rinse off the blood and dirt, stopping again under each streetlamp, to look at the blood on my shoes and clothes. I was sure it could easily have been taken for oil. Not that it mattered. I knew nobody would see me.

At the end of the street, near the car park, a large house stood detached from the others, in its own grounds. It was a Georgian house – it had been painted pink, and was half-obscured by a hedge of chamaecyparis. Someone inside was listening to music; I recognised the piece, and I stopped to listen. The singer was Elizabeth Schwarzkopf, and I felt a wave of emotion, a mixture of joy and regret, a sense of the beauty and transience of the world. I knew I was being sentimental, but that did not detract from the poignancy of the moment. I pushed open the wrought-iron gate and stepped into the garden to listen. The front garden was paved, like a courtyard, but it contained a number of large containers of evergreen shrubs, camellias and rhododendrons, tensed with bud, wrapped in a cold film of frost. There was a square stone pool on one side, surrounded by coloured flagstones. It was filled with thirty or more Japanese carp, far too many for the size of the pool, crowded together like opium smokers, golden and red, their plump bodies hanging in the water, almost motionless. I stood there, in a stranger's garden, gazing at them. They seemed to me utterly amazing: miraculous, absurd presences, suspended in the black water. I wondered what would happen to them when the really hard frosts came, when the water froze and they lay helpless, in their sleeves of ice, or pressed to the hard bed of the pool, unable to disappear into the mud.

As I drove home, it began to snow, slowly at first, then heavy and quick, filling the windscreen till I could barely see the road ahead. By the time I reached the edge of town, it had begun to settle, fledging the trees and the empty fields on either side, augmenting the distance between one familiar object and the next, till the landscape seemed wider and emptier than before. I was tired now; I could hardly see the road, and I found it difficult to drive after I had left the streetlamps of Weston behind me. At one point, I pulled into a lay-by and sat in the car with the engine running. My watch had stopped. More than an hour had passed since the episode in the churchyard – maybe two hours – but it felt like minutes. I was surprised at how much it had affected me. Not long before I had been elated, filled with energy, convinced that what I had done was a logical necessity. Now I was exhausted, and the whole thing seemed arbitrary and absurd. I got out of the car and walked a few yards in the thick snow: I wanted to be out in the open, to breathe the cold air and think. I was parked on the highest point of the road, on a ridge looking down over the partly wooded valley. I could see the lights of a farmhouse at the foot of the slope and it occurred to me that this was the house that had once belonged to a friend of my parents. I had even visited there as a small boy, one Sunday afternoon in winter. All of a sudden I had a vivid memory of standing in the hall in a bow tie and flannel trousers, waiting for someone to take my coat. It must have been Christmas: I could smell mince pies and my fingers were tingling with frost. The memory was instantaneous and clear: a long hallway led to the kitchen, at the back of the house, a large painting of a horse hung on the wall to the right of the door, a wooden staircase rose into the darkness. I was trying to remember the name of my host, a man about my father's age, whose wife had died young – Thompson, Thomason – when, in my mind's eye, a light came on above me and a girl slowly descended the stairs. Helen Thompsett. She was carrying something. I couldn't see what it was, but I knew there was an object in her hand. For some reason, I had the idea that it was a candle.

Now the house belonged to someone else. I had no idea where Helen was. It was the first time I had thought about her in twenty years, but now I could see her clearly: her hair was dark-brown, tied back with a pale blue ribbon; she would have been two or three years older than me then; she was dressed for a party, in blue satin. I could see her eyes, they were the same deep-blue colour as her dress. I had been in love with her for a while; perhaps it had even begun that evening, though I hardly ever saw her, she attended a girls' school on the other side of the county, and only ever came home in the holidays. I had probably only seen her three or four times, once for that evening around Christmas and on the rare visits she and her father made to our house, but I could see her clearly in my mind's eye: radiant, mysterious, unbelievably beautiful. For one absurd moment, a wave of regret passed through my body, a truly physical sensation, like sudden blood loss, or vertigo. I wanted desperately to go back to that moment, to see her descending those stairs again, to have power over time. Once, in childhood, I had read a story where a boy has the ability to move through time, because of a magic word he has learned from an ancient Persian scholar. For several months, I really believed this word existed.

In the farm below, someone was out in the yard, moving about with a torch or a lamp. The house was lit too: these were the only lights I could see across the whole valley, though I knew there were two or three cottages further along the single-track lane that ran down from the main road to the farm. Above the lights, the woods were filling quickly with snow. I stood a while, watching it fall, and I tried to imagine that I was looking back into the past. I imagined, if I drove on to the junction and found that narrow road, I could drive down into the yard where Mother was leaving the house, laughing softly, calling goodnight to the people behind her and I was turning back for a last glance at Helen, too shy to speak, or even wave.

Things were falling apart. My sense of elation had completely disappeared, and I was beginning to be afraid, wondering if the body had been found, if I had left any clues. Maybe the Stanley knife had fallen out of my pocket during the scuffle, and now it was lying there in the dark, covered with my fingerprints, a few feet from the body. For a moment, I even considered the absurd idea of going back and checking to see if I had left it behind, but

I managed to put that notion out of my mind. I got back into the car and drove on, peering over the wheel to see my way in the snow. I had to move slowly: the snow on the road was thick and fresh, and I could hear it crunching under the tyres. I repeated a list of words I had memorised years before, a list of place names from Canada. I was surprised I still remembered so many. I had liked the Indian words, because they seemed old and rounded, like stones smoothed in a riverbed, but some of the new names were beautiful too, with their suggestion of a new life, and the promises the settlers had made to themselves as they wandered in handfuls across the country: Vermilion Bay; Fort Hope; Fort Resolution. I was tired now, and it was hard work concentrating. At one point, an animal — a dog, or a fox — ran across the beam of my headlamps and I hit the brakes, skidding slightly, though there was no danger of hitting the creature, I was moving so slowly and it was so far ahead it had been and gone before I could even tell what it was.

That night I hid my bloodstained clothes in the shed and bathed thoroughly as soon as I got home. Lillian was still asleep when I slipped in beside her. I remember thinking how lucky it was that she slept so deeply. The next day I checked the car and washed away some traces of blood, then I drove back to Weston. I parked in the usual place and began walking slowly in the direction of the library. When I reached the churchyard entrance, I found it closed. There were four policemen in uniform, and several other men in civilian clothes; they were searching the grounds, wandering up and down between the headstones in the early afternoon sunlight. Much of the snow had thawed here, but patches remained in places, in the shadow of the hedge and around some of the shrubs by the graves. A small crowd had gathered by the gate to watch, casual shoppers and office workers on their lunch breaks, hoping to catch a glimpse of the murder weapon. There was a small tent pitched near the steps, where I assumed the body was concealed. I was a little surprised, as I thought Jimmy had fallen a little further away.

I stopped and joined the other watchers. I was surprised that nobody tried to move us on, the way they do in the films. I half-expected a gruff, good-natured constable to wander across and wave his arms, telling us all to go home, that there was nothing to see, that it was all over. Instead, the men in the churchyard ignored us: they were going about their business, a little bored, perhaps, yet suitably thorough, systematic in their approach, as any professional will be when he is being observed at work, treading a fine line between complacency and interest, maintaining the appropriate gravity of the position. One man, who seemed to be charged with watching the crowd for any potential interloper, stood next to the thin plastic tape that was stretched across the entrance to the churchyard. From time to time he glanced at a young woman by the gatepost, and gave her small, shy smiles, which she returned brightly. He was younger than the other men, and had grown a moustache to seem older, but this only had the effect of exaggerating his youth. It amused me, I must admit, despite my anxiety about the knife, to imagine these two people flirting at the scene of my crime. I lingered for a few minutes, half-hoping the policeman would speak; perhaps he was too conscious of his position, perhaps he was just shy, but he did no more than smile for a few minutes longer, and after a while the girl moved off with her friends, presumably to get back to work. I glanced at my watch. It was one thirty. I considered whether it was correct to ask the young policeman what had happened, or whether this was expressing too much of an interest. I didn't want to draw unnecessary attention to myself, yet it seemed a harmless enough question. Suddenly, I heard a voice at my shoulder, and I turned to find the librarian, Miss Patterson, standing beside me.

'Hello,' she said, smiling brightly. 'We haven't seen you for a while.'

From the slight sharpness in her tone, I assumed she had not yet forgiven me for deserting her library.

'Hello,' I replied, innocently. 'How nice to see you. Is the library closed?'

'Not at all,' she said, laughing a little too readily. 'I don't actually live there, you know, though it sometimes seems that way.'

I smiled to show appreciation of her dedication, and her self-deprecating sense of humour.

'What's going on?' I asked, with obvious, and slightly impolite curiosity.

'Ah.' Miss Patterson came reluctantly to the matter at hand. 'They seem to have found a corpse.'

She pronounced the word with some relish, like someone who has been allowed, after a lifetime of abstinence, to enjoy some dark pleasure.

I reacted appropriately.

'A corpse? Here? I'm sorry, I—'

'A body,' she interrupted. 'Everyone seems to think it's a murder.'

'I see.' I allowed a moment for thought. 'Do you know who it is?'

'The murderer?'

'The body.'

'Ah.' She smiled with grim satisfaction. 'They think it was one of the vagrants. You know the ones. They came into the library once, when you were there.'

'Oh.' I nodded. It didn't seem appropriate to show concern or sympathy with the victim. Miss Patterson obviously had none.

'What's happening now?' I asked her.

'They're searching the grounds,' she said.

'What for?'

'The weapon, I suppose.'

'Have they found anything.'

She shook her head.

'Not while I've been here. It's not really very interesting, as a matter of fact. Just some tramp. Maybe he wasn't murdered at all. You know how people are.'

She gave me a sidelong glance.

'I don't suppose you're much interested in the affairs of some dead tramp, anyway,' she said.

I nodded agreement.

'Not much. Still, it's a little inconvenient.'

'Well, I look at it this way.' Miss Patterson replied, 'As far as I'm concerned, these people are mostly just a nuisance. They come into the library to get warm and they frighten people. They sit around begging. It's just one less disturbance to worry about.'

'Quite,' I said, curtly. I noticed that the young policeman had overheard Miss Patterson's last remark and was watching her out of the corner of his eye. I think he had something he wanted to say, but again, he stuck to his duties.

I loitered a few moments longer, then excused myself. Miss Patterson offered to walk with me to the library, but I told her I had to go back for something. As soon as I reached the car park, I got into the car and drove away. I was already regretting my weakness. Even if the police did find the Stanley knife, there was no possibility of their tracing it to me. The only obvious danger was of my losing my nerve and attracting attention to myself.

In any investigation, the real detective is the suspect. He is the one who provides the clues, he is the one who gives himself away. As long as I remained calm, and treated the problem as a question of logic, I would be quite safe.

I kept an eye on the papers for a while, but the news was thin. The police had found the body of a homeless man in the church grounds, they did suspect foul play, but they had no clue as to the murderer's identity or motive. They questioned Jimmy's former associates; for a while, it looked as if they were going to charge one of the men I had seen him with, that day in the pub, but nothing further emerged and eventually the story dried up. I kept the papers out of Lillian's sight, even though I knew she couldn't read them, and there were no photographs of the murder victim. I didn't want to take any risks of upsetting her now.

As the weeks and months passed, she grew strange and awkward, as if she were some creature I had fished from the sea. The swelling on her belly looked alien and uncomfortable in a body as thin as hers, it was too local, it did not seem to belong to her body, and her skin changed colour suddenly, from its usual rose-white to a shade of vellum. She was tired all the time. I have always been suspicious of the phrase, *the glow of pregnancy*, and my suspicions were only confirmed by Lillian's appearance. Instead of a glow, her whole body seemed to become more and more dull, sallow and sickly-sweet and vague, like a candle burning out or a line of smudged writing. Nevertheless, she remained cheerful. She tried to continue with her work around the house, even when I assured her that I could look after things. Sometimes she spent whole days in bed, watching television. It appeared that her happiness was too large, too strong to be affected by a temporary physical setback. I think

I was more affected by the change in her appearance than she was. I found a book in Mother's library which described what happened during pregnancy; I found another that showed how a child was delivered, by conventional methods and by Caesarean. This was invaluable. When it came time, I would be obliged to manage the delivery myself.

I did all I could to make Lillian comfortable over those last few months. I had no idea, of course, that I was about to lose her, but I am glad I treated her so well, looking after her when she was sick, finding the kinds of food she could bear to eat, tending to her when she was too tired to get up. I feel better now, when I think how happy she was for that little time. And there were moments, even towards the end of the pregnancy, when she seemed beautiful to me, in spite of everything, moments when she seemed perfectly balanced, immersed in a cool white light, almost incandescent. Whenever I remember her, I will see her like that, just as she was before the twins were born.

The day came. I had been waiting for the moment with a mixture of dread and anticipation. On the one hand, I was afraid for Lillian, and for the child; on the other, I wanted to observe this bizarre process, I wanted to see how a body worked when giving birth. To be honest, I was mystified by everything I had read, how sometimes the head is too large for the birth canal; how, sometimes, small incisions must be made between the anus and the vagina, to allow it to pass through; how the child will sometimes turn around and come feet first; how the birth can be so difficult that a section of the woman's belly must be lifted, in order to free it. Even the easier births might demand the use of forceps to pull the child free, with the risk of damage to the head, or even the brain, if too much force were applied. It seemed to me that the whole process was too complicated, too unnatural, as if humans had not been intended to give birth at all.

I was apprehensive, naturally, about the possibility of having to cut Lillian when the time came; obviously a Caesarean, or any other complex surgical procedure was out of the question. Yet, as it happened, the birth was relatively easy. She seemed to suffer some pain, but she was patient, stoical, even brave – especially when, after the first child emerged, I felt something else was there, inside her, and I realised the child I had just prised loose had a twin.

In spite of her bravery, the process of giving birth to twins damaged Lillian badly. Afterwards, she would not stop bleeding: the blood was thick and dark, and I was worried that she would lose too much and become ill, or die. After several hours, however, the bleeding stopped and, though Lillian was too weak and tired to feed the twins, I managed to keep her and them well through their ordeal. Or so I imagined. I have no idea, now, what would have happened if Lillian had survived. The experiment would have taken quite a different course, naturally; perhaps the outcome would have been different, under different circumstances. Not that there is any profit, ever, in speculation. There is only one possible course through life, and that is the course one takes. No other decisions could have been taken, no other circumstances could have arisen.

The next morning, Lillian developed a fever. The children were unaffected, but she was still unable to feed them, and I had to continue with a compound feed. Fortunately, I had stocked up on feeding material, in case such difficulties arose. I had also set up a temporary crib arrangement in the spare room, which was fortunately large enough to take both children, so that, while I was involved with tending to Lillian, they were never left alone. They had one another for company. Perhaps that was where their extreme attachment began. Perhaps it was not nature after all, that made them as they were. It might just have been the circumstances of those first few days, when they lay as close together in the world as they had done in the womb. Strangely, for new-born children, I don't remember their crying very much. They seemed hushed, awed, as if they were aware, with some residue of womb-knowledge, of their mother's condition. I was certain Lillian had contracted a serious infection, and I considered taking her to a hospital. Her condition seemed to worsen by the hour, and she began to bleed again. Needless to say, it was a difficult time. For the first time, I considered the possibility that Lillian might die, and it was a delicate process, getting the twins established on the feed compound. I am surprised, now, that they survived that stage.

I watched Lillian closely. Her symptoms were dramatic: extreme pain, fever, tenderness in her stomach and belly. I soon realised that my first guess had been correct; she was suffering from an infection of some kind, worsened no doubt by the dramatic loss of blood over the first few hours. Once again, I considered calling a doctor, but I convinced myself that it was too dangerous. To call a doctor in would not only jeopardise the future of our experiment, it would also link me, through Lillian, to Jimmy. It wasn't just one life that was in danger, it was everything: my life, Lillian's new-found happiness, our whole enterprise. If I had brought in medical help, I might have saved Lillian's life, but that would have been all. She would have been taken away from me, and placed in an institution, where she would, most certainly, have been unhappy, perhaps even subject to the kind of abuse she had suffered before she met me. She was a girl who had probably been abused all her life. Without me, she would be helpless. Wherever she went, a Jimmy would appear and take over. There were thousands of Jimmys.

As a matter of conscience, however, I asked her what she wanted me to do. I told her to nod if she wanted me to take her to the hospital, and shake her head if she wanted to stay with me. I explained that, if she went to the hospital, I couldn't stay with her anymore, but that someone else would look after her and the twins. She shook her head.

For the next couple of days, I convinced myself that she could pull through. She was in terrible pain – that was obvious – but she seemed to have the will to fight. I had found some antibiotics amongst Mother's medicines, and I administered these till they ran out. I don't know how much good they did. After a while, she began to sink, and I realised she wasn't going to make it. All that remained was to make her as comfortable as possible, and prepare her for what was to come.

I have always admired the literature of the Tibetan Buddhists. They alone have understood the power of language in manipulating, not only this world, but the world beyond this, the world between one world and another, the *bardo*, the otherwise silent reaches of limbo. What could be more appropriate, I thought, than to use the Tibetan Book of the Dead to ease Lillian's passing from this life to the next. It was, in a sense, the ultimate power of the word: the story was there to guide the soul through death, to sustain its awareness of itself, as it was dislodged from one state and hurled forward into another. So it was that, on the last night of her life, I sat down by Lillian's bed and began to read. I had read her stories before; I had read her poems and fairy tales only recently, during her illness, but this was different. I began at the beginning and continued reading far into the night. When the pain was too great, I dabbed her face with a damp cloth and let her sip a little water, but I did not allow the course of the reading to be interrupted. I am certain that it helped her. I don't know how much she understood, but there are different levels, different ways of understanding. Of course, she suffered a great deal: that was inevitable. When she died, just before dawn, she had lapsed into a semi-conscious state; by then, I think she was less aware of what was going on.

It is a mistake to mourn the dead. I know that now. It makes no sense. We keep ourselves occupied, forgetting our own mortality, as if we possessed a unique form of presence, a unique reality, but what we also forget is the reality of the dead. It's as if the living were more real for being present – yet there's no logic in that position, it admits too much of transience. When Mother died, it didn't make her any less real. On the contrary, it fixed her forever in a single moment, a perfect attitude. When Lillian died, she seemed as real to me as she had been, living. The words I was speaking brought her into focus during those last several hours: I think she knew what I was doing, even if she didn't understand at an intellectual level, and I think she was glad. I know she smiled when I came to the part where the body of the departed becomes a rainbow, then finds itself in paradise, amongst the angels. I think she was ready to die, then. One part of her knew what was happening, and accepted its fate. For my part, I was able to let her go easily, without regret.

What is the scientist? This is the most important question. I am not talking about the people who play at the edge of science, whose loyalties are to other powers, to home and family, to self, to business. They are the ones who talk about ethics, but they do not possess the true scientific ethic, which is total commitment. The scientist is the one for whom everything is a hypothesis, the one who is wholly dedicated to the experiment. There can be no exceptions. Although I can say, quite truthfully, that I had become fond of Lillian, although I missed her in the weeks after her death, I never once allowed myself to compromise the experiment for her sake. I could easily have taken her to a hospital and handed over the responsibility for her life to someone else. Instead, I did all I could to save her and, when that failed, I let her go. To have done otherwise would have meant betraying the experiment and, probably, betraying her. I do not believe, even now, that she would have wanted me to allow that to happen. The night after she died, I laid her out in one of the dresses I had bought her, on our first shopping trip. She looked utterly at peace. I carried her out to the grave I had prepared for her, in the new iris bed, and I laid her thin body in the cold earth. Before I covered her up, I kissed her, once, on the mouth. She had become a part of something larger than herself, larger than either of us, and I was sad, for a moment, that I had never been able to tell her that. It seemed a shame, that she would never know what part the twins might possibly play in the development of ideas. It seemed a shame, that she couldn't have had one glimpse into the future, and become aware of the possibilities it presented.

part three

the twins

I knew from the first that it was an error to think of the twins as *my* children, whatever the biological reality. It's only a flaw in the language that confuses kinship with possession, and in this case the kinship was accidental. I had no real connection with these creatures who lay in the basement room, crying and fouling themselves, clinging to a life that I could easily have ended with a basin of water or a length of twine. For a few days after she died, Lillian was a palpable absence in the house, a stain that lingered over the makeshift cot before it faded away, almost imperceptibly. After that she was gone. It was simple, uncomplicated. Nevertheless, I was aware that the twins had been responsible, not only for her death, but also for the pain she had suffered, and for that reason alone, I was free of any instinctive sense of kinship, any desire to protect or nurture them that I might otherwise have possessed. I had read about such things – how, even in the most unexpected circumstances, a kind of paternal instinct would be aroused by the sight of one's offspring, but from the start, the twins were, quite rightly, nothing more to me than laboratory animals. I had become fond of Lillian, in my way. I had enjoyed having her around the house; I had enjoyed waking in the dark and finding her thin body beside me, warm and lithe, like an animal, and in factual terms, they were her children. Nevertheless, I had no difficulty

145

in proceeding with the experiment. The only difficulty was in keeping them alive and well for the first few weeks, so they might be of use later. I had to spend a fair amount of time and money fitting out the basement room as their permanent home and, at the same time, a suitable laboratory for my observations. To avoid the risk of discovery, I was obliged to do all the work myself. I built them a pen in the basement, so they could be contained easily later. I placed an observation grille in the door, I set up tape machines and video recorders in the room itself, so I could keep them under observation at all times. I knew I would have to ensure they were fed and cleaned, but otherwise I wanted to stay out of the basement as much as I could. It was an essential part of the experiment that they remain isolated. With the recording equipment, I could observe them without intruding into their awareness, just as wildlife photographers observe young chimpanzees at play. The essential point was to create a suitable environment, so they would be deprived of nothing essential to their development. I wanted them healthy, to ensure that my conclusions would not be clouded by any other factors. It was hardly surprising, for instance, that Genie had initially failed to develop intellectually, given the filth and squalor in which she lived. By contrast, the twins would have everything they needed. Everything except language. To avoid any residual possibility of attachment, or of accidentally speaking in their presence, I decided to give them labels rather than names: A for the male, and B for the female. That way, I would always be aware that they were, in essence, laboratory animals, not humans, and certainly not my children.

The following months passed slowly. I recorded every observation, every sign of development, each gesture, each scream, in my log book. The twins passed quickly through all the stages of infancy that I had read about. In text book

terms, they developed normally: eyes, teeth and, as far as I could
tell, hearing. Soon they were able to move about on the floor,
playing with their toys, displaying surprise and wonderment, fear
and pleasure, a need for contact. They were obviously aware of
one another from an early stage. They vocalised freely, as babies
do. At fixed times each day, I provided them with music –
Mozart and Bach, but no vocal or choral works – in order to
aid the development of their intelligence. For purely scientific
reasons, the records I kept at this time are very detailed, but
I wasn't particularly interested in the early stages: I fed them,
changed them, kept them clean and waited for that critical
moment when, if they were going to speak, they would begin.
I wore a surgical mask when I was obliged to handle them: first,
to avoid passing on bacteria, and so infecting them with disease,
which was a greater risk than it would have been otherwise,
given their abnormal situation; second, to avoid their seeing
me as anything other than a keeper. I didn't want them to
see me as a parent, or even as another of their kind. I had
read books where all manner of creatures, ducks or geese, for
example, would latch on to any available parent figure, even
when that figure was of a different species. It was important
that the twins did not see me in that light – and it appeared that
the mask worked. Generally, while they were aware of me, they
did not seem to regard my existence as anything more significant
than the light in the room, or the music from the stereo system
I had set up on high shelves on one wall of the basement. When
I was forced to handle them – and I did so as infrequently as
I could – they usually cried; most of the time, however, they
were too wrapped up in one another to notice me. Their sense
of attachment was extreme. Mistakenly, I believed that this was
a good sign; perhaps I was thinking fondly of Poto and Cabenga.
There had never been a control experiment in that case, after

all. If the private language they had created was based on the
snatches of German and English they had heard, that was only
because they'd had such material to hand. What if there had
been no such material? I wondered if I was about to find out.

The singing began late one evening, just after feeding time,
when I had dimmed the lights and left the room, so they could
rest. At night I normally left the tape machine running, with
one cassette in the deck, so I could monitor them until they
fell asleep. Thus, if anything out of the ordinary happened, I
would be aware of it, even when I was away from my listening
post. Until that night, the tape had revealed nothing out of the
ordinary: usually no more than a random cry, or a series of
gurgles through the quiet hiss of the machine. Often there
was nothing – no sound, no movement. As far as I could tell
without a control, the twins were quiet for their age, though
not abnormally so. They had vocalised in the usual way – or
at least, in the way I would have expected. I had no reason to
suspect they were holding anything back, and I had no cause
for imagining they were deficient as subjects in any way. Yet
until that night I felt there was something, if not wrong, then
not quite right, something almost eerie about them, and I
wondered what they were thinking and feeling, when they lay
together, not yet asleep, but utterly silent, utterly motionless.
It was absurd, of course, but from the start, I suspected them
vaguely of a conspiracy of some kind.

The events of that night changed everything. From my
records, I see that they were exactly eleven months old at
this time, which, in retrospect, seems extraordinary. I had
expected language, if it happened at all, to come somewhat
later; more slowly, in fact, than language development in a
normal environment. Yet that night, and on the five or six

nights following, they moved from almost total silence to a near-constant singing. It came out of nowhere, with no provocation, no stimulus, that I was aware of. One day they were mute infants, the next they had something extraordinary, which pleased and excited them from the very first.

It must have begun quite soon after I left the room. For some minutes they were still then, slowly, almost tentatively at first, they began to vocalise in a different way, taking turns to utter phrases in a soft, haunting singsong that seemed, on a first hearing, a form of improvisation, an exchange on which they were working together, in a hesitant exploration of the possibilities of sound. To begin with it was experimental, almost quizzical, but after a frighteningly short time the singing grew louder and more confident. At the same time, it was more complex, with the twins joining together then moving apart in a kind of counterpoint till, by the time the tape ended, they were already on the way to developing an elaborate, seemingly conversational music. I have to admit that, the next morning, when I reviewed the tape, I found this music utterly beautiful and, from the first, I was certain that something was concealed in those sounds, some logic or pattern quite alien to the sense I knew. I was convinced there was a structure that I could find, in the usual way, by a slow and devoted analysis.

Now, when I look back on those early days, I wonder where things began to go wrong. One mistake I made – and this surprises me, even now – was to assume, at the deepest level of my thinking, that the principal use of language was to convey information. At the surface, of course, I understood the social functions of speech. I knew that most discourse was pretty well meaningless when subject to analysis. Most people, for much of the time, use language as a crude tool: as a means of defence, or a medium of self-affirmation, or a social lubricant. A great deal of talk is aimless. There are times when people speak only to reassure themselves that they exist, or to validate the existence of others. Without language, they might lapse into an uneasy solipsism, unsure of the point at which one thing ended and another began; stripped of their boundaries, they would begin confusing themselves with the world around them. They feel they must speak, and it doesn't matter very much what the speaking is about.

Of course, there is something a little despicable about this need for small talk. Its ugliness is offensive: the nonsensical exchanges one hears in restaurants, or in theatre queues – they are all so unnecessary, so aesthetically redundant. I remember once, as a change from driving everywhere, I made a long train journey northwards. It was a clear, bright summer's day: for part of the journey the railway line ran along a stretch of coastline, and I sat in my window seat, gazing out at dark rocks and a wide, empty expanse of shore, at thin veils of water spread over bright wet sand, where a mass of wading birds were hunting for sandworms, stepping out carefully over the glistening silt beds, as if they had just arrived, of a sudden, in a new world: a world that, for them, was mysterious and enchanted, a world that, all things considered, must seem to any thinking mind a logical impossibility. A crude evolutionist would say this world came into being by chance, by a series of random accidents, but even a moment's thought will confirm that the statistical probabilities of each of these tiny accidents of weather and genetics happening, not only one at a time, but also as part of a complex and delicate whole, are extremely remote. The very existence of anything seemed to me, on that journey, a breathtaking and terrifying miracle – yet the other people on the train treated the whole magical event as something banal, ignoring the light, the sky, and the glittering water, hanging over their seats to chat to their companions, playing word games, droning on about nothing, repeating to strangers the same dull stories they had always repeated, to anyone who would listen, expressing their opinions, mumbling received ideas and half-truths to one another as if they were passing on items of arcane wisdom, or the cryptic messages of an oracle. As they hurtled on through this shimmering landscape, surrounded by wonder – a wonder, moreover, that they had no reason to believe would persist from one moment to the next – nobody looked at the world. Nobody saw it. At one point, a bird – a great tit, I think – flew up alongside the train, dipping and rising, flying along in perfect parallel for two or three hundred yards before turning and flicking away into the bright air. Nobody noticed. Instead, they talked: on and on, they talked about nothing, unravelling the world in their tedious, ugly converse.

This is the nature of social existence. We talk in order to impose limits, to contain the world in a narrow frame. Yet every textbook on language proceeds upon an assumption of communication, concerning itself with structure and grammar, with meaningful exchange, with the possibility of analysis. There is almost no mention of this simple making of noise – even though that is the reason for most speech. People talk in order to make a noise, and so be. Manners demand that they say something meaningful, at some level, but they might as well grunt, or howl.

So, knowing this, why did I assume the twins were conversing? Why did I ever imagine their song was anything more than their way of being in the world, a simple extension of the cries and gurgles they had made as infants? Why did I never seriously suspect that singing was their way of telling themselves and one another that they existed, or even more likely, was the sole strategy they had open to them of casting a veil over all they saw and heard, over every feeling, every flicker and ripple of the world around them, every unexpected change in their own bodies and minds? Why did I imagine they had minds at all, in the real sense of the term. Birds sing. Foxes bark. Dolphins send variable and complex messages across miles of ocean. That doesn't mean they can think. It was an error to assume that the singing of these children was any more valid than a cock's crow at dawn, or a seagull's mocking laugh.

Nevertheless, it was an assumption I did make, for no good reason. I believed the twins were more than animals – more, I believed they were real in a way that the other people I encountered were not. For some reason, I believed they experienced their world with a sensitivity I could only imagine, and it troubled me. In the end, I recorded an open verdict on the twins. Nothing was proven one way or the other by the experiment I carried out. Yet in my heart I knew by the end that they were talking to one another about a world I could not see, or hear, or touch, and the language they were using was so perfect, so fully attuned to their being, that it was beyond any analysis that I might attempt.

For a long time, they lived together entirely, hardly losing sight of one another. They were only physically parted when I took one twin out of the pen to feed or bathe it. From the beginning, this was a distressing experience for them both. A, in particular, cried and struggled desperately whenever I took him away from his sister. After a while, they became slightly more able to cope with separation, but I never kept them apart for longer than was absolutely necessary. Looking back, I see this was probably a mistake, but it did not occur to me that there would be any profit in parting them, and it made life a good deal easier to keep them together. As they grew, they vocalised constantly when they were alone, chanting to one another in their odd singsong and, despite my confusion as to the nature of the song, I was excited. I thought this a good signal for their future development towards language. It didn't strike me as odd that, whenever I entered the room, they fell silent. Perhaps I felt this was nothing more than an obvious animal caution. I suppose I was still thinking of Poto and Cabenga. The possibility of their developing a private language out of this song beguiled me: if it happened, I could stay clear of them for about ninety per cent of the time, and observe their progress without their knowing, using the video camera and the tape recorders. They could not be aware that their attempts to exclude me were useless.

One afternoon, however, I decided, as an experiment, to remove one child from the pen and take it outside into the garden. By this time they were around fourteen months old, and I felt it ought to be possible to part them, if only for an hour. I chose B, because she seemed the more independent of the two. After the months of confinement, I wanted to see how she would react to the space and the light of the outside world.

As usual, the child's body stiffened when I picked her up, but she did not cry out, she simply struggled against my hands like a small animal. She kept her face turned away, looking back at the pen, where A sat, flailing his arms in silence. It was no different from all the times I had taken her from the pen to bathe or feed her, until I opened the door. As soon as she could no longer see her twin brother, her body slumped and, for one terrible moment, I thought she had literally died in my arms. It was a moment before I realised she was only playing possum. For the first time, I felt a twinge of resentment at the implication that I was a danger to her.

She remained limp and silent till we reached the stairs. Then her body tensed again and, flexing her arms and legs, she tried to break free, to lever herself out of my grasp. I was surprised at how strong she was. I held her tightly and made my way to the back door. It was a struggle to get it open and hold her still at the same time; I ended up tipping her head forward and holding her with one arm around my waist, while I turned the doorknob with my free hand. B screamed once, at the top of her voice, then the fresh air and the light hit us, and she jerked her head up to see what was going on. From where we were standing, we could see the garden: the dark green of the holly trees on either side of the path, the iris beds in full flower, the paler green of the pleached apple trees against the back wall. The sudden riot of colour must have startled her, or perhaps it was the sudden light; nevertheless, I turned her body around and, gripping her tightly with both hands, I lifted her up so she could see clearly. I had wanted to show her the garden, to let her experience a new stimulus, but she only screamed again then, as I held her still, slumped into the same state of apathy as before, like a baby monkey that has been parted from its mother. I cradled her in my arms and looked into her face. Her eyes were half-open, but she wasn't seeing anything. By an effort of will, she had closed down her mind. It was uncanny. In a matter of moments, as we stood there in the afternoon sunlight, she became inert, quite lifeless, utterly withdrawn. For the first time, I began to be aware that keeping them together and allowing them to develop so closely might have been a mistake. They were too intertwined. It was as if they were one person. What if it were true that twins could share their thoughts, with no need for ordered communication at all? Their singing might be nothing more than play, or an attempt to mask the real exchanges that were going on under the surface, exchanges so subtle I would never be able to penetrate them.

In retrospect, I realise that I lost track of the experiment at this point. I had intervened unnecessarily, caught up in a fantasy that, by showing one twin a world wider than that inhabited by her brother, I might induce a change of some kind – perhaps a development of their language, or a break of some kind that might allow me a way into their experience. I was unscientific in my approach, I was looking for something that wasn't there, and missing what was. I had lost sight of the larger picture. The behaviour of the twins confused me: their development was too rapid, the singing was too intricate, too complex, their attachment to one another a red herring that I allowed to distract me. At the time, I wanted to see an order, a structure in their song that was not present. I believe, now, that there was structure, there was even meaning, but not in a form that I could understand. Meanwhile, I was bound by the grammar I understood. I was like a man who sits at a window and looks out at the world: he cannot move, he cannot even turn his head to the side, and all he can see is a brick wall, or a patch of sea, or a corn field, and he thinks the entire world is one undifferentiated brick wall, or sea, or corn field. He cannot imagine diversity, because the only basis he has for imagining a world is the evidence of his eyes. If, as he stares at the brick wall, he notices how the light changes, how sometimes it is redder, or more yellow, or turns black, he might understand that something else exists to cause this transformation, or he might decide that one of the properties of this wall is that of changing its colour on a more or less regular basis, and the rest of the world, the rest of that infinite brick wall, possesses that same property. If, as he sits there, head fixed, eyes trained on the wall, he hears a train, or the cry of a gull, or a child singing, he imagines these sounds are also properties of the wall. If he could turn and look at himself, or at the room behind him, or the chair in which he sits, he might come to understand more of the nature of things – but he cannot. He is so fixed upon the wall, that he sees nothing else.

In one respect, at least, I was this man. I had my eyes fixed upon a structure, an idea of order, which I believed must, *of necessity*, be universal. I was like the child who draws a tree, who shows a trunk and a leafy crown, a scrawl of brown and green, an asymmetrical lollipop shape, cut off at the bottom, where the trunk of the tree meets the earth. If I had focused on the whole picture, I would have resembled the botanical artist who observes the tree when it has fallen, or who plucks a blade of grass from the earth and draws the roots, and the creeping stems that emerge from each individual plant. I would have seen a symmetry, a deeper order, a more complex and subtle world.

Yet, in another way, I believe my error lay in a kind of passivity. Separating the twins was nothing more than an act of frustration: until that moment I had made no connections, I had never looked closely enough, I had failed to discover the whole picture. I believed that the scientist is the one who observes, who does not interfere, but simply records the data and waits to find the pattern that emerges. If nothing becomes apparent, the assumption is that nothing is there, or nothing that can be described. It was a failure of imagination of the kind that the great scientists would not have tolerated in themselves. Yet, given that it was so impulsive, my intervention was equally unacceptable. As the weeks passed, as the children had developed their song, I had sat patiently and waited, like someone working on a simple puzzle, who believes that everything can be investigated by his normal methods, everything can be described in the accustomed terms.

The twins developed alarmingly. Physically, they were progressing in advance of any expectations I might have had, given their age, and the restrictions of their environment. But it was in their singing that I noticed the most obvious development. Sometimes they vocalised for hours on end, but there was always a freshness about it, an air of improvisation, a freedom that seemed to delight them. I have no clear idea whether the pleasure arose from listening to what the other was saying, or in the making of their own sounds. Maybe it was a mixture of the two. I kept making and analysing the recordings, but I had more or less given up hope of ever breaking the code and, after a while, the singing began to haunt me. I could hear it throughout the house; I even heard it in the evenings, long after I had shut them away in their pen and gone out into the garden. Even when I played music to drown it out, it persisted, like tinnitus. I wanted to know what it meant. I wanted to play the tapes to some complete stranger, to see if I was missing something. Sometimes I told myself that it was no more than an animal form of communication, like the language of dolphins, a rich vocabulary of musical tones and dynamics that were too alien for me to interpret, as arcane as the bee's dance, that appeared so noisy and erratic, yet conveyed the precise positions of flower beds and clover leys. Yet what could they be telling one another about the world outside, about the position of the sun, or distant meadows, or schools of herring?

I listened to the tapes over and over again. I looked for patterns, but there was nothing I could detect. As far as I could tell, there were sounds that never came up twice in all the recordings I had; others were repeated all the time. The code, if there was a code, was impossible to crack, unless you knew the basic rules, the parts of speech, the syntax. There was no evidence of a vocabulary.

For a long time, I looked for myself in their exchanges: if the singing meant anything at all, I thought, it would surely contain one sound, a special tone or sequence to denote my presence, some constant that would indicate whatever it was they felt for the masked creature who brought them food and drink, who bathed and changed them, the large, inexplicable presence who possessed such power in their small world. I thought this must be the starting point: if I could find myself in their discourse, I would find the key to unlock their secret. Yet, when I analysed the tapes, isolating those occasions when I came in to the room, from the exchanges before I entered to the exchanges that occurred after I left, I could find nothing consistent. They were always silent while I was there. They might have been singing to one another for hours before I appeared, but as soon as they heard the key turn in the lock, they broke off. Then, as soon as I had left, they resumed their singing, but there was nothing to show that they were making any reference to me.

I was discouraged by this fact. I felt as if I had lost something, as if I had become invisible. I really began to feel that I had stopped existing a little. Now I understood why parents taught their children those words first: Mamma, Daddy, Mum, Mummy, Dad, John, Mary – whatever they asked to be called, however they saw themselves in their children's eyes, it was one proof of their being, an ontological victory, when the child looked up and spoke the appropriate word for the first time – recognising, making certain, becoming complicit. Parents vied for that moment. I had made real efforts to maintain objectivity, to keep my distance; yet, in the end, I have to confess that I succumbed to the most maudlin of emotions. It troubled me, to be excluded from their world. They wouldn't even sing while I was in the room, even though they knew – and I was certain they knew – that I could not understand.

I worked hopelessly on the doomed experiment for several

months more. I would not allow myself to discard the idea that some form of communication was taking place, which meant it was susceptible to analysis, but in the end, it was stalemate. I considered teaching them a single word, to see what would happen. I thought of playing them tapes of people speaking, in a number of different languages, those sample tapes you can send away for, with a few basic sentences of French, German, Italian, Spanish, Greek. Or I might just turn on the radio and let them listen for a while. From a few words, they might still construct a whole language, as Poto and Cabenga had done. It was the last option: the twins had never heard human speech other than their own. I decided I would expose them to language somehow, obliquely, without comment, then observe the results. To begin with, I played vocal works during their daily music sessions: German lieder, Breton folk songs, Tibetan chants, sung masses. I made a conscious decision to avoid English, though there was no logical reason for doing so.

It made no difference. They listened to the voices – and it appeared they were registering something new – but they continued to sing as before, whenever they were alone. I played spoken word tapes, extracts from plays, readings of poetry, recipes, instructions, conversations. They ignored these. While they would often stop singing to listen to what I played, they seemed not to notice the speaking voices, or, if they did, they felt no interest in them.

One afternoon I stopped the tape abruptly and waited to see if I had their attention. Then I began playing one of the first tapes I had made of them singing together, several months before. They sat entranced, enraptured, listening closely. I had no idea if they knew what it was they were hearing, if they knew it was their own voices coming from the speakers. Yet, from their expressions, I guessed that this was the first time they had truly understood that the world is an inhabited place. I think, now, that they were always looking for others of their kind, but all they could see was a wall, a set of speakers, the bars of a pen, a door. Suddenly, after a few minutes of listening, they began to sing back to the tape, back to themselves, in a pure ecstasy of recognition. It was unbearable. I allowed them to converse with themselves for a while, then I couldn't take it any longer. Hoping they would not notice me, I opened the door quietly and stepped into the room.

They stopped singing as suddenly as they had begun, and looked at me. The recorded voices continued to echo around the walls of the basement room, like the voices of ghosts. Using the remote, I stopped the tape. The expression on their faces was identical: it was the shame of having been discovered, of having, by some weakness, betrayed themselves to me. For the first time, I was real to them. They could see me, they could not help but see me and I felt a surge of triumph, as if I had slipped through the one crack in their defences. I wanted them to know I had been listening all along, that they had made a mistake, they had no secrets from me, but the only way I could do it was to repeat back to them what they had just sung. I rewound the tape and replayed a short section, then, with my head tilted slightly to one side, I tried to reproduce the sound, singing softly, as they did, watching their faces all the while. They stared at me. They seemed surprised and I thought, for a moment, that I had beaten them. Then, as I played back another section, and sang again, more sure of myself this time, more accurate, they glanced at one another and began to laugh, the way children do when somebody makes a mistake or says something foolish. And yet it was a kind laughter. It wasn't resentful or mocking. Something had collapsed, in that moment of surprise, and I suspect they were seeing me for the first time. For the first time, I think, they understood that I was like them; but at the same time, utterly strange, someone to pity a little, in the same way as we pity a fool, or a madman with delusions of grandeur. From that day on, they did not bother to stop singing when I entered the room. They sensed my coming, but now they knew there was no need for secrecy. Now, as I had so ably demonstrated, there was no risk of my eavesdropping on their conversations. Now they knew, once and for all, that I couldn't speak their language. Now they had decided, once and for all, that I did not exist.

Looking back at my notes, I see now that I was becoming delirious. The solitude was wearing me down – that and the constant singing, and the suspicion I had, from time to time, that I was being observed. I had no good reason for this feeling, yet I felt it, and even recorded it in my observations, as if it had some relevance to the course of the experiment. It was around this time, in fact, that my notes ran wild: they were highly personal in places, sometimes absurdly metaphysical, occasionally maudlin. One entry, made towards the end, runs as follows.

I know now that what matters is what we choose to consider. All of life is a process of selection: we filter out the irrelevant details in order to come at a truth of sorts, which is no more valid than another possible truth, except in the fact that we selected it, as opposed to something else – and language is the instrument of that process. What matters is not just the story that is told, to ourselves and others, but the way the story is told, the words we select to convey, and to solidify, our vision. Standing in the kitchen tonight, as darkness fell, I saw that I could think of Mother, dying in her white bed, or I could have thought of Lillian's small, bewildered cries of pain and fear, as I guided her away into death. I could think of the twins in their unassailable world. I could ask myself what

*choices they are making, what world it is they are constructing.
Or I could fill a glass with water and be amazed by the very
fact of surface tension, amazed by the very existence of things
in liquid form. I could walk outside into the garden and look up
at the sky. It doesn't matter who I am, or what I have done.
I am nothing other than a mind in space, noticing each detail
then moving on, noticing then forgetting, looking then moving
on. This is all there is: a vast, endless stream of random events
– stars, thoughts, spiders, rain, buildings, children, money, lava,
blood, sex, pain. Each mind makes what it can of the data but no
one can say what sense is. No one can say, with conviction, that
one thing is entirely true, while another is false. It doesn't work
that way. When I stop like this, when I stand still and see it
all streaming towards me, my own mind empties. The order is
coming from somewhere else, and I don't know what it is. At
times like this, language is meaningless. People talk about God,
or time, or the great unified field theory, but these are nonsense
words. If I allow myself to experience the world fully, I can see
that there are no descriptions. Is this what the twins know? Is
this why they see, and forgive, me?*

It was the hottest summer in years. I barely slept; when I did, I
had strange or violent dreams that woke me suddenly in the dark
and left me uneasy. I felt close to fever. The twins seemed not to
notice the heat: now that they were old enough, I would risk
taking them outside with me on some evenings, carrying them
one at a time into the garden and letting them play around at
my feet while I watered the beds. As long as they were together,
being outside seemed to encourage their physical development.
In the basement room, they had never got past crawling, in the
narrow confines of their pen. Occasionally, B had managed to
stand, tottering on her feet a moment before she collapsed into

a sitting position again, with a small thud. Out in the garden, they developed by leaps and bounds. I suppose, given the right environment, they were only too ready to make up for lost time. I made no effort to help them: I didn't teach them to walk, they simply helped one another. It was as if they had both had a bright idea, at exactly the same moment, and had worked out the mechanics of the thing for themselves. I was always amazed at how well they did, as soon as they put their minds to something. It was as if their wills were united, as if they had become one. In the end, that was the cause of their downfall. They got a sense of their own power, and I had to cut them down.

One night they broke free. I still have no idea of what happened. I was asleep in my room, having one of those feverish dreams that seemed to mean so little when I woke and analysed them, yet left me feeling uncomfortable and anxious, in a way most nightmares would not. In this dream, I was walking along a country lane, in the middle of summer. The dream was filled with the same oppressive bright heat that filled the waking day: the road was narrow and dark, tall banks of hogweed and nettles grew up around me on either side and I could feel something moving along beside me in the undergrowth. I could feel it, I could even hear it breathing, but I couldn't see it. I kept trying to make it out in the dark foliage, but whenever I stopped, it vanished, there was no sound, no movement, only the still beds of weeds, sticky with honeydew and cuckoo-spit. Then, finally, I caught a glimpse of it, out of the corner of my eye. It was utterly hideous: an immense damp-haired creature, with a dark, piglike face, and it seemed ready to attack.

A moment later, everything had changed. I was standing in the hall of my own house, but the furniture and pictures I had known all my life had been replaced with ugly knick-knacks and bric-a-brac, of the sort found in junk shops. It was perfectly still, a clear summer's day. I could smell the flowers in the garden, I could see the sunlight flickering on the polished floor. I walked to the foot of the stairs and stood listening. Upstairs, someone was crying, a woman, or perhaps a child – I couldn't be sure – and, suddenly, I was afraid. I ran outside, back into the light, and began walking away from the house as quickly as I could. But I had only walked a few yards when I heard someone calling my name and, when I turned back, I saw a woman running towards me, with a letter in her outstretched hand. I could tell from her face that the letter contained bad news and I wanted to call out, to make her stop, but when I opened my mouth, no sound came. As the woman came closer, I saw that her face was a blank, there were no features, no eyes, no mouth, only a mask of white skin.

I woke in the dark. The room was still, but someone else was there. I could feel it; I had that sense of being watched. I sat up quickly and fumbled for the bedside light.

It was the twins. They were standing in the doorway, eight feet away, in their night clothes, bolt upright, as if standing to attention, or perhaps just trying to stay balanced. I had no idea how long they had been there, or how they had escaped from the basement. I was certain I had locked their door before coming upstairs; but there they were, standing side by side, watching me intently. When I switched on the lamp, they didn't flinch: it was as if they could see as well in the light as the darkness. It was some time before I noticed that they were soaking wet, as if they had just come in from a rainstorm. They seemed very sure of themselves; they did not resemble toddlers at all. They were more like wild animals, silken and wet and attuned to the night, and there was something about them, some latent power, that froze me. I think for a moment I half-expected them to attack, but they did not move; they simply stood in the doorway, staring.

It was a difficult moment. I was aware of the fact that I had been dreaming, that I might have talked or cried out in my sleep. What if they had done this before, if they had come to my room and spied on me, then left without my knowing? I hadn't found the basement door open, or even unlocked, but in all the time they had been there, I might have left it open without even realising it. If I had made that mistake, I could easily have made any number of others. The one thing that was established, beyond doubt, was that I had allowed them to escape on this one occasion. Where one error is found, you are bound to assume others have gone unnoticed. If they had heard me speak, if they had heard something other than the abstractions on the language tapes, the experiment was finally ruined, and I still had an idea that something could still be salvaged from this experiment. I was conscious of the fact that I had almost cried out, involuntarily, a moment before, when I had caught sight of them standing there, watching me in the dark. I needed to know what they had seen and heard, most of all, I needed to know how they had come to be standing there, soaking wet, on a warm summer's night. I was horrified by the thought that they might have made their way out into the world somehow, where they would have been discovered. I had a picture of them, in my mind, wandering unsteadily along the road, in the summer moonlight. Yet what troubled me the most was something I hadn't really registered at first, something that felt like a false memory, and I might have been mistaken but, later, when I recalled switching on the lamp and seeing them there, I was certain that, for the first time ever, in my presence at least, they were smiling.

★   ★   ★

With the benefit of hindsight, I see that it was at that point, with that mistake, that the experiment with the twins ended. I couldn't trust myself any longer; I couldn't make even the most basic of assumptions. From that day on, whenever I went out, I would worry that I had left the door unlocked and, at that very moment, they were clambering up from the basement, or stumbling out into the light of day, making instinctively for the gate that led to the road. It was absurd, I knew, but whenever I left the house, I would leave the car running in the drive and go back to check, to see if everything was secure. At first it was just the door I checked; then I would stop to be sure I could see them both, safely locked up inside. Then I began to check the whole house: gas, water taps, electrical points. I had fantasies of fire breaking out while I was gone. A kettle had been left on, it had shorted, the fire had begun in the kitchen and swept through the house – it was only a matter of luck that a passer-by had spotted the flames and called the fire brigade who had, in turn, rescued the twins. I had fantasies of flood. At one point, I started going back two or three times to be absolutely certain. Once, in the supermarket, I left my trolley in the frozen food aisle and drove home in the rain, because I was convinced I had left the key to the basement room in the door. When I returned, my trolley was gone.

It was an absurd situation. It wasn't only that I was concerned the twins might escape. The fact was, their very existence had begun to affect me in all kinds of ways. It's hard to believe, now, that I was afraid of them, but I was. Whenever I went down to the basement, I felt sick and dizzy, as if I had been poisoned, or I was suffering from an allergy of some kind. I only had to look at the twins, playing together in their pen, to feel a wave of revulsion sweep through my whole body. It was a familiar sensation. I had experienced it before, I knew, and I racked my memory to remember when. Finally, I recalled the day my father found the cat and brought it home, without a word of warning. It was something I would never have expected from him. The small, rather ugly creature he carried into the hall wasn't even a kitten, it was just a youngish cat he'd picked up from a refuge, one of those cat protection places, where lost and misbegotten creatures end up, like the souls in limbo, waiting to be redeemed. I remember him now, standing in the doorway, with the cat in his arms; he hadn't even asked for a box, or a cage, he must have just selected it, more or less at random, then picked it up and carried it away.

It was almost Christmas. He had been sitting around in the kitchen for days, waiting for snow and listening to the songs on the radio – 'White Christmas', 'Winter Wonderland' – the sort of sentimental nonsense Mother couldn't stand. I can see, looking back, that he must have been going through a crisis of some kind: he appeared more distant and unreal to me than ever, and I vaguely remember an impression I had that he was thinking something through, trying to come to a meaningful conclusion. He kept drifting into the downstairs study, where Mother and I would be sitting, reading, or talking quietly; he would stand at the window and look out for long minutes at a time, then he would say that he wished it would snow. I couldn't see what difference snow would make, one way or another, but it was evident that it mattered to him. He must have said it a dozen times or more. Maybe he was trying to remember something from his childhood, and he thought snow would help. Most of the time, Mother ignored this performance but, for a while at least, I was a little intrigued.

Finally, a few days before Christmas, he went out early in the day, and came home around tea-time with a thin, red and white cat. He made a pretence of giving it to me; he said it would do

me good to have a pet to make friends with and look after. I
stood watching, in utter disbelief, as he released the scrawny,
grimy-looking animal into the clean, perfect space of our front
hall. Then I turned to Mother. I was certain she would forbid
him to keep the cat in the house but, to my surprise, she simply
walked slowly upstairs to her own study, without uttering a
word. My father seemed not to notice; he took off his coat
and led the cat through to the kitchen, where he found a bowl
– a bowl for humans, something Mother might have used – and
setting it down on the floor, filled it with milk. The cat inched
forward cautiously, sniffed at the edge of the bowl, then turned
away and began exploring the kitchen, rubbing itself up against
every surface, leaving its mark, making our house its own.

'I suppose he doesn't want his milk,' my father said, looking
at me kindly, assuming my interest, including me against
my will.

'I suppose not,' I said, as dryly as I could manage. I couldn't
understand why Mother hadn't acted. Two words from her,
and the cat would have been gone.

'I've got some food in the car,' my father said. 'I'll fetch it.'

He stood a moment, gazing at me. He seemed to expect me
to participate, to stroke the cat, or pay it some kind of attention,
or perhaps volunteer to feed it. I didn't say anything. He went
back outside, without his coat, and returned a moment later,
with a cardboard box full of tinned cat food. He opened one
tin, fetched another bowl, then took a fork from the drawer and
half-filled the bowl with the dark, foul-smelling meat. When
he set the meal on the floor, the cat ran to it immediately and
began to feed. That was when I began to feel ill. It started with
a knot in my stomach, then dizziness, and I experienced that
same sense of personal invasion that comes when you have
a stomach bug, or a severe cold. Something from outside –

something animal – enters and takes control, depriving your body of its natural autonomy. I was being forced into the most distasteful intimacy. It was evident that my father wanted me to like the cat, that any sign of revulsion on my part would be a rejection, not of the animal, but of him. Yet the longer I stood there, in the warm kitchen, watching this scrawny, somehow parasitic creature eating from Mother's crockery, the longer I was exposed to the smell, to the sounds it made in feeding, the worse I felt, and I knew, immediately, that I had to do something to protect myself, and Mother, from the consequences of my father's folly.

Christmas had never been extravagantly observed in our house. Mother disliked sentimentality. My father would buy me several gifts and, on Christmas morning, he would present Mother with a single, discreetly-wrapped package, which she always set aside unopened. I never knew what it was. Generally, however, the whole occasion was over by breakfast-time. Normal order was restored; I put away the toys and books my father had bought me and Mother prepared a light lunch. We did not subscribe to turkey and funny hats, though my parents sometimes had guests on Boxing Day, for drinks, or supper. They always behaved discreetly, omitting any mention of the actual occasion from their conversation, as if they had simply happened over by chance, or on an ordinary invitation.

That year, it was different. We had a large tree, with lights and decorations, and I was perplexed to see Mother taking part, helping my father to dress the tree and hang up decorations, standing in the kitchen, making mince pies and angel cakes. The cat looked on, not quite certain if the occasion was a matter for fear, or for fascination. Though my father claimed he had brought the creature home for me, he was the only one who paid it any attention. He was the one who decided it should be called Rusty, because of its odd colouring; he was the one who fed it and let it out from time to time, standing at the kitchen door to see that it did not stray too far, then going out and calling it in, when he felt it had been outside long enough. Mother had decided to pretend the creature did not exist: I was so convinced of her power that I imagined, for several days, that the animal would sense her rejection and slip away some afternoon, leaving my father at the door, calling out to an empty garden. Instead, Rusty made Mother the central focus of its existence: wherever she went it followed; whenever she appeared, it woke up and went to her, making soft mewing sounds. It must have cost Mother some effort of will to ignore it, but my father, who ought to have been jealous, was pleased.

'Rusty likes you,' he would say, grinning at Mother, as if he had just solved a long-term problem, or discovered the answer to a question that had been troubling him for years. Mother wouldn't answer. She simply kept up the pretence that the cat did not exist, no matter what, even when it tried to jump into her lap, or when it attempted to rub against her legs, smearing her with its scent, making her a piece of its territory. For hours at a time, she would retire to the upstairs study, where the cat was not permitted. It didn't take long for me to understand that she felt the same sickness at the pit of her stomach, the same slight giddiness that I suffered, whenever the animal was close. For my father's sake, I didn't really want to hurt the cat, but in the end I had no choice. For Mother's sanity, and for my own, I had to do something.

When I returned to school, after that strange Christmas, I found a book about domestic animals in the library. Immediately, I turned to the entry on cats and began a careful study of the subject. I looked at the bone structure, I read about its capacity for night vision, but what I found most interesting, and promising, was the fact that the sense of smell is integral to a cat's being. I read that every cat had small glands on its body which emitted a uniquely-scented oil, with which the animal would mark its territory, leaving its signature wherever it went. Thus every cat had its own scent, by which it recognised itself; it followed, then, that that scent was its very identity. I was fascinated. For animals, any sense of self they had was defined by something external, by the presence of their body oils on rocks and trees and patches of ground around a given territory. Take away the scent, I reasoned, and the animal was lost. Its own territory, even its body, would become alien and threatening.

The possibilities for experimentation were infinite. It would have been most interesting, for example, if I had been able to substitute one cat's scent glands for another's, and observe the results. I could imagine the animal's confusion, perhaps a kind of madness, as its sense of itself was dissipated – it be would like waking up in a new skin, with a different face, a different body. What would happen, I wondered, if a male's scent-glands were replaced by a female's? Would its behaviour change? It was just one of a number of fascinating questions, and I regretted the fact that such an experiment was beyond my capabilities. What I could do, however, was to try to mask Rusty's natural scent, to remove his sense of identity. That, in itself, would surely be a disorienting experience and it might possibly drive the animal away. I didn't really want to kill it, to begin with, at least. I was sure, if I could make it leave, someone else would find it and take it in. People are sentimental about cats and dogs, they treat them as they would treat other humans. Better, in fact. They love animals, because animals can be anything you want them to be. They cannot talk.

A few days later, when my father was away on business, I set the experiment in motion. It was a crude affair. I mixed up a cocktail of Mother's perfumes in an old pump-action rose sprayer, then lured Rusty into the shed. The cat wasn't suspicious: I had never given it cause to be wary of me, and it was relatively easy to lead it inside and lock the door behind us. I made it think I wanted to play, waving a length of cotton around in front of its nose; then, when I had its confidence, I trailed the cotton into a wooden box, where Mother usually kept plant pots, and eventually managed to trap the animal inside, by covering the box with a large garden sieve and weighting it down. Rusty made no serious attempt to escape; it must have imagined this was part of the game. As I started to administer the spray, it began to panic, but there was no escaping the box, and I had plenty of time to douse it thoroughly with the alien scent. I sprayed it several times, trying to cover the whole body, to mask the creature from itself utterly. It occurred to me that, without its scent, a cat might imagine it was invisible. It would be like the experience a human might have, if he looked into a mirror and saw no reflection.

Finally I stepped back, let the sieve fall, and opened the door. The cat scrambled quickly out of the box and fled out into the garden. I had tried to be careful not to spray near the eyes or the mouth, and I was reasonably sure I hadn't caused any real injury; nevertheless, as soon as it was outside, it began to cry horribly. It sounded like a child crying, as if, somewhere behind that flat, whiskered face, there was a human soul, trapped in the mind and body of an animal. I had read how some peoples believe that souls pass from one form to another after death, how a man could become a dog, or a rabbit, or a horse, depending on the actions of his life, his sins and errors, the moments of kindness and betrayal, the loves and fears he had endured – and maybe it was true, maybe there was a soul trapped in that cat's body, something more or less human, yet diminished in some way, a form that was somehow degraded, part-instinct, part-consciousness. Maybe that was another reason why some people wanted animals around them; maybe they saw traces of people like themselves in those dumb, appealing eyes. Maybe that was what my father had seen in Rusty. He had caught a glimpse of himself in this pitiful form, and he had reached out to give comfort – to the animal, to himself, to everything that was weak and needy. The idea disgusted me. There is nothing worse, nothing more distasteful than pity. Rusty had wandered away into the far corner of the garden, and was now standing by the pear tree. It was still crying softly to itself, and the sound irritated and enraged me. I shouted at it to stop, but that made no difference. Then, after two or three minutes had passed, and it still had not stopped, I went back into the shed and fetched a spade. The cat didn't try to escape. I hit it once, then I struck several more times – I can't remember how many – till I knew it was dead. I hadn't planned to harm it, but for that one moment, I had no choice; I had to expunge that scrap of living misery, to destroy its pitiful soul. There was something about it that made me sick to the stomach. Even if it had run away, even if I had never seen it again, I couldn't bear to think of its continued existence.

Now that same sickness had returned with the twins. There was something about them that transcended the gap between human and animal. They seemed to exist in both states at once, plugged into a current of instinct and blood-knowledge, communicating through song, each enjoying the other's warmth and scent, as an animal might, with the same creature subtlety. In one sense, they weren't human. They were aware of things that I could not detect; they lived on a different plane. I couldn't even guess at the nature of their world. I had already decided that I would never be able to decipher their songs. Perhaps they were meaningless; perhaps their meaning was so different from what I would think of as meaning, that it could hardly be seen as meaning at all. Yet they seemed to know me: even when they had ignored me, during those first months, they must have been watching me all along. That night I woke and found them at my bedroom door, gazing at me in silence, I was aware of a new self-assurance, a contained malevolence that gave them real, animal pleasure. And, suddenly, I understood that I was afraid of them. It was fear that caused the sensation in the pit of my stomach, fear that made me dizzy, just as it was fear that had sickened me when my father brought Rusty home. I can see, now, that it was quite irrational, but after that night, I was always afraid the twins would attack me in some unexpected way, just as I had been afraid that my father's cat might, at any time and without provocation, steal into my bed and sink its teeth into my throat.

It was too hot to sleep. I had lain awake for over two hours, under a single white sheet: the heat had made me a little feverish, every time I moved, the entire surface of my skin rippled with tiny shivers and waves of sensation. I kept imagining I could hear the twins, deep in the basement, singing to one another, or climbing the stairs quietly, making for my bed. Finally, I went down and fixed myself a cold drink; then I walked from room to room, peering into each moonlit space as if it were somewhere entirely new, a stranger's house where I had woken up by chance. As long as I was moving, I heard nothing but the chinking of ice in my glass, a sound like tiny bells wrapped in the faint lapping of water; but every time I stopped, every time I paused to listen, I tuned in, once more, to an endless current of creaks and shifts, and that distant music which, the more I tried to convince myself it wasn't there, the more I strained to hear

it. I descended the basement stairs in the dark and stood at the
door. I could see nothing through the grille. I switched on the
microphone system. The twins were asleep: their breathing was
soft and regular, and they were so attuned, each to the other, that
it might have been one child sleeping in that dark pen. I think
I was a little jealous of them then. Together, they were more
individual than I would ever be. Even though they were totally
dependent on one another, or perhaps because they were, they
defined one another perfectly: for each of them, the world was
filtered through the other's eyes. There could be no sensation
that was not tinged by their feelings for one another. I had been
sure of that ever since I'd heard them laughing together. They
were complicit. Maybe that was the reason for their singing –
they weren't conversing, as such, they were simply performing a
ritual of confirmation, a celebration of their combined existence.
The complicity that existed between them suggested a world
that I was incapable of experiencing, and some of the pleasure
of being in that world, part of their private joy, was predicated
upon my exclusion. It was as if I was the one who could not
speak; as if, for me, the world was nothing more than a jumble of
meaningless and disquieting sensations – and it came to me, then,
that I was the one who had been placed in the Dumb House.

After that, I was ill for several days. At some point, I fell asleep
in a chair, and sat drifting between the day's long heat and some
distant winter of the mind, a journey through dark woods fuzzed
with snow and strange, miniature towns, like the towns in naive
paintings, all iced bridges and steeples and people skating on the
rivers. I had some idea in my head, something to do with parallel
lines, and how they meet at infinity. It was as if I was trying to
formulate an idea, some hypothesis that would explain the very
order of the world, how it was inherent in all things, yet was

essentially inexpressible, or transparent to common sense, like the finer points of mathematics. I suppose I was suffering from a kind of fever. Yet, somewhere in my mind, these wanderings seemed part of the experiment to me, a vital stage, as vital as the records I kept, or the hypotheses I had formed.

When I woke, the room was buzzing with flies. I had been asleep a long time, perhaps days: the lamp was still lit, the dust burning slightly, and I caught a trace of a faint fleshy smell, like the smell of a hospital sick room. No doubt the flies had been drawn to the light, sensing an escape then finding only another room, another set of walls, another puzzling window to beat against. My fever was going now, but my throat and mouth were very dry, as if I had swallowed sand, and I still felt disoriented. I had the sensation of having been wrenched out of my body, of only just finding a way back. For a few seconds, I had the strong impression that I had just seen myself from the outside, a man sitting in a chair, like a character in a film – and I didn't know who it was I was looking at. The image stayed in my mind a moment, still vivid, still real, then it faded. Yet, even for that short time, I was aware of something else, aware of myself, listening for the twins, before I even remembered their existence. That was when I realised fully that they were responsible for my fever, they were the ones who had made me ill, that night, when they came to my room. It was wholly illogical, but I was sure, in that moment, that they had willed my sickness. I could still see their eyes watching me, their silence held; I could feel their complicity against me, utterly malevolent and vengeful. There was no question that their development had been unnaturally rapid over the last two or three months. As they grew, their minds were becoming stronger, more united and I knew, if I did not break their power, they would become too powerful to contain.

I went to bed. I needed to recover my strength, so I could deal with the problem. After all, I told myself, there was no point in becoming hysterical. I understood the dangers of total solitude, coupled with prolonged exposure to some extremely irritating stimulus. I'd read about experiments on war prisoners, where a subject would be kept in solitary confinement for weeks at a time, with no other ambient sound than a tape loop of white noise. Much sooner than expected, the subject begins to experience hallucinations, delusions, prolonged bouts of hysteria. He hears voices. He loses all sense of himself; there are no boundaries between him and the rest of the world. After a few days, the experimenters could turn off the tape and the subject would go on hearing the same sounds, only now his anxiety increases, because there are moments when he becomes aware of the silence, because he no longer knows what is true and what is false. What I needed was to break out of that cycle. I was even on the point of leaving the twins in the basement for a few days, just to get away, to drive to the coast and listen to the sea, or go for a long walk in the hills, to hear the wind, the sheep in the fields, the skylarks. But I couldn't leave them. It was a ridiculous fear but, even though I knew they were nothing more than a pair of small children, I was certain that if I abandoned them to their own devices they would escape, and the experiment would be exposed.

That was when it came to me – that night, as I lay, in the still heat, straining to hear something that wasn't there. It made perfect sense: it would be a new stage of the experiment, it might even provide a new insight, the very breakthrough I needed. The question was: what would happen if one of the twins could no longer sing, if one voice was suddenly turned off? How would they react? Would they try to devise some other means of communication? Was it communication? As far as turning off a voice went, I knew it could be done. I could crush the larynx from the outside, or I could open the neck and sever the vocal cords, or even remove the larynx entirely. I knew that much from my medical text books. I also knew the experiment would be hazardous: crushing might cause asphyxiation, and my skills as a surgeon were limited, in spite of my experience in dissection. Even if the operation was successful, there was a possibility that the children would lapse into that state of apathy I had observed when I tried to part them. By now I believed, with utter conviction, that their continued existence depended on their ability to communicate with one another. They weren't individuals in their own right; they were the two parts of a single entity. That would always be so. That was the reason for my lack of progress: the twins were isolated in their own fortress of sound, and I could not enter, no matter how hard I tried. If one of them could no longer speak, they might try some other method of communicating, something I could interpret; or the one who remained might turn to me, in order to go on living, and then I might break the code, if any code was there. Besides, if things went wrong, if the experiment failed, nothing would be lost. The twins' song had become unbearable to me.

Of course, I probably knew the outcome all along. By then, I could not escape the feeling that I had failed. It was a completely unscientific attitude: no experiment ever fails, it can only be conducted, observed and recorded. I thought of Michelson and Morley, whose work on the speed of light and the nature of the ether led to Einstein's discovery of relativity. In science, there are no dead ends. Yet Michelson and Morley were horrified by what they considered the failure of their enterprise; they were Christian men, horrified at the vacuum, the flaw in the fabric of the universe that their observations seemed to expose.

There were nights when I lay awake for hours, thinking of opportunities I had missed. There is no more powerful fantasy than the fantasy of what might have been. I could see, with regard to the experiment, that any fault was mine, but now I wanted to destroy the twins and begin again, with a single subject, as the experiment had demanded all along. My mistake had been to keep the two of them together. It was time to resolve the situation, to clear the way for something new.

I began work the following morning. I decided B would be the better subject for surgery. She was physically stronger, and I thought she would have a better chance of survival. I had several books on human anatomy and surgery in the library and I studied them carefully before I started. In my nocturnal meanderings, I had already realised that there were really only three options to consider: temporary disabling of the vocal cords, for example, by the exertion of pressure around the larynx, with the attendant danger of asphyxiation; a laryngotomy, where the vocal cords are severed *in situ*; or a full laryngectomy, in which the entire larynx is removed. There was no doubt in my mind that the latter would prove fatal to a child. The simplest approach would be to crush the larynx in some way, effecting a temporary, or even permanent loss of speech, but that seemed too crude, too ugly. I decided to investigate the laryngotomy option further. It seemed within my capabilities, no more difficult than some of the experiments I had carried out on mice and rabbits, and there was something attractive about the idea of opening the child's larynx and looking inside.

According to my surgery textbook, laryngotomy is a relatively straightforward operation – technically, at least. The difficulties would arise during aftercare: B would experience some distress, and I would have to take measures to ensure the wound did not become infected. There was also the problem of the anaesthetic. I could use some of the drugs Mother had been prescribed, or perhaps alcohol to at least immobilise the child during the operation, but I would have to research very carefully the amounts I could use without causing long-term damage. Also, the twins would have to be kept apart for several days and I had no idea how they would take it. Nevertheless, the experiment was destined to end inconclusively if I did not act, and I was curious to see if B's larynx was different from the norm, if it had become altered by the constant singing, if there had been some kind of adaptation. However I looked at it, the decision was a reasonable one. Even if B died, I would still have A and, once he had recovered from the separation trauma, we could begin the experiment again, on a new basis. Then again, if he really could not live without his sister, or if I felt the experiment had been irretrievably compromised, there was no shortage of young, homeless women on the streets of every major city in the country. I reflected on how easy it had been to get Lillian to come with me: I had exerted no force, and very little persuasion. All I had to do was find someone similar, someone who was desperate for food and safety, and show her a modicum of kindness – and the experiment could begin again, with a new subject. I would learn from my mistakes with the twins. Nothing would be wasted.

I used some of mother's old drugs to put B to sleep. I administered them with her food, while she was still in the basement room then, when she was close to unconscious, I carried her upstairs to the study, where the operation would take place. A became distressed as soon as he saw B going under, even more so when I picked up what, for him, might have looked like her dead body, and carried her from the room. I was concerned, of course, but there was nothing I could do to reassure him, and my time was limited. I have to confess, also, that I was excited by the prospect of performing the operation.

I remember once, in school, we were studying poetry for an examination. The teacher was telling us how the key to the poet's thinking lay in a single phrase, something about how dissection is murder; how, as soon as you chose to dissect a living thing, you lost its essence, something bled away, something invisible. The teacher, Miss Matheson, seemed to agree with the writer: the more she talked about nature, and the soul, and immortality, the happier she became. Finally, I raised my hand.

'Luke?'

I liked Miss Matheson. She was pretty, and she had a way of saying your name in class, as if she was surprised at your very existence, as if the recognition that you were present was a real pleasure for her. There was a kind of appeal there, too; she wanted us all to join in, to feel the same way about poetry as she did. I asked my question.

'Where is the soul, Miss Matheson?'

She smiled.

'That's a good question, Luke,' she said. 'That's exactly what the poet is trying to tell us.'

She paused for effect. I remember noticing how pretty she looked, standing by the window, in the afternoon sunlight. She was wearing a pleated tartan skirt, and a white blouse, with a red cardigan over her shoulders, hanging a little loosely, as if she had just pulled it on.

'You can't pinpoint the soul, ' she said. 'You can't just cut a flower or a laboratory rat open and find its essence. All you will see are petals and sepals, bones and blood vessels and organs. The real life of things can't be seen under a microscope.'

'Then how do you know it exists?' I asked.

She smiled again.

'Well,' she said, 'we all know there's more to life than bones and brain cells. There's thought. There's beauty. There's personality. What the poet is saying is, you can't take up a scalpel or a magnifying glass and go looking for those things. Science only shows us how the machinery works. It can't tell us why the machine exists, or anything about what lives inside.'

I nodded. I liked watching her talk, and I wanted her to continue, standing there with the light on her face and hair, her hands moving in the still air as if she were performing a magic trick. I didn't agree with a word she said; as far as I could see, that poet she admired so much was an aberration. The very image of the thinking individual, ever since the Renaissance, was of a mind overcome by curiosity, descending into crypts and cellars, risking death or exile in order to open and examine and draw the cadavers of suicides, or the newly-executed. Mother had given me books that showed the artists working by candlelight in the cold mortuaries. All anyone knew for sure about the human body was there, in Leonardo's drawings, or in the flayed bodies that Vesalius drew, as if they were statues, posing in classical landscapes with their tendons, or muscles, or arteries exposed. If the dissectors had obeyed the laws of their day, we would still be throwing our waste into the streets, people would still be dying of plague or diphtheria in Paris and Milan. The sick would die slowly, in dark, foul-smelling rooms, covered with leeches and lance-marks. Throughout history, the important discoveries were made by those who ventured upon the unspeakable. I knew it was so, even then, and I wanted to stay behind after the class, to tell Miss Matheson what I knew. I suppose I wanted to impress her, too. I can see that. Looking back, I understand that all I wanted from her was a reaction of some kind, even if it was nothing more than shock, or dismay. Yet, when the moment came, all I could say was that I didn't agree with the poet, that I thought science was the most valuable tool we had, if we wanted to know the world. Miss Matheson smiled that smile of hers, and I fled in confusion.

Now, as I prepared my instruments and set out the study for the operation, I saw that I had entered upon that domain of the unspeakable. I had always understood that the human skin was the true frontier. I had dissected animals, but I had never cut into human flesh. Now, as I strapped B to the table and applied the sterilant to the area around the larynx, I considered that immaculate, unbroken surface. I had planned everything. I intended to make the smallest possible incision, to open the skin and tissue around the larynx and, with the minimum of trauma, sever the vocal cords on both sides. This was the most delicate work, a surgical exercise in which I could take real satisfaction; also, the very act of breaking the skin, of entering another human body, intrigued and excited me. I could see why people might kill for that sensation, simply to enter and explore this forbidden region of blood and cartilage and tissue. Such people would be the victims of an exquisite curiosity. They would be haunted by the mystery that existed only a knife's depth away. As long as we imagine the body as wet and messy, a sack of offal and bile, this desire may never arise. It takes someone with faith in a near-angelic order of things to want to enter another body. Such a person would have to believe in a silent and imperceptible order: not God and his angels, nothing mystical – rather, something entirely scientific: an informing principle, the presence of a spirit that might be detected in every pattern the body revealed. Maybe Miss Matheson was right: there is a soul, there is something that inhabits the body, something that cannot be isolated in the meat of the brain, or the chambers of

183

the heart. Yet it would still be visible, in the sheer beauty and economy of the human body, in the sheer beauty and economy of all matter. Whatever you decided to call it – soul, or mind, or spirit – something as fine as mist was present in the flesh: not soul, but what the Greeks and the Gospel of Saint John called Logos, a universal and impersonal order, informing everything according to its nature. The key was there: order is neutral. The operation I was about to perform was more than a physical investigation, it was a metaphysical enquiry into that universal order. Perhaps this metaphysical – this religious – element is present in any act of dissection, if it is performed in the correct frame of mind. Perhaps it is even present in dismemberment. Perhaps every incision is an act of spiritual love. As I fastened B's head in place and raised my scalpel, I half-believed I would find something unexpected; some filament of preternatural warmth, some subtlety of design, lodged in her throat like a key.

Everything has its own, peculiar sound: skin; cartilage; vein; the natural flow of living blood. It surprised me. I had worked on living bodies before, but this time it was different. This time, the body was human. For minutes at a time, I felt as if I was working on my own body, slitting open my own skin and clamping it back, peering into my own larynx. Compared to this, every dissection and investigation I had ever performed was the exploration of inanimate matter. Now, for the first time, I felt I was working on a living soul. As soon as I made the incision – I was elated to discover that my hand was steady, that I made no errors – I was aware of the warmth and the movement within. Everything had its own sound and its own colour. Nothing was quite as I expected, despite my researches. Everything was lighter, finer, more distinct than I had thought possible. At the same time, I was more aware than ever of the meatiness of the flesh. When I saw the larynx – that beautiful mechanism, almost birdlike in its delicacy – I was still aware that the nerves, the finely-modified cartilage, the perfectly-adapted muscles were immersed in flesh. At that moment I was aware of an overwhelming sympathy: no matter how carefully it was done, the severing of the vocal cords, with the attendant damage to the larynx itself, seemed more an act of violence than a piece of surgery. I had the sensation in my own throat, of two fine elastic strings, snapping with a sudden jolt, and I had to steady myself to make the next tiny incisions and finish the job. I had to remind myself of my purpose, then. Having come so far, I told myself, there was no stopping on what were, mostly, sentimental grounds.

I worked carefully, yet I finished much sooner than I had expected. The vocal cords were fine and easily severed; after that, I experienced a wave of satisfaction and relief, and the suturing was fairly straightforward. I had a difficult moment when the child moved suddenly, just as I was putting the last stitches in, and I was afraid she would regain full consciousness before I could finish. I realised I hadn't thought this part of the operation through in full; I'd been too busy thinking about the incisions and the care needed to sever the vocal cords without inflicting too much damage. I had made sure I knew where everything was: the layrnx, the vocal cords, the major arteries. I had studied the problems of after-care: the possible breathing problems, the trauma, the need to protect against infection. When, at last, I had completed my work, and B showed no signs of waking, I carried her into the spare room and placed her in my old cot. Then, exhausted, I got cleaned up, went down to the kitchen, and made myself a pot of coffee. I must have fallen asleep in my chair; when I woke it felt as if a few minutes had passed, at most, but, when I glanced up at the window, I saw that it was dark outside. I ran upstairs to the spare room. B was awake. When I switched on the light she moved her head a little, but she did not look at me. She looked at the light bulb for a few seconds, then she turned her face to the wall. She was expressionless. She didn't cry, she didn't even seem to be in pain. She was remote, uninvolved, like some animal in the zoo that refuses to acknowledge the existence of its observers. I checked to see if the dressing was clean and intact. I had considered the danger of her putting her hands to her throat and opening the wound anew, but everything looked fine. Feeling more reassured, I fetched the portable CD player from the study, put on Tallis' *Spem in Alium*, and set it to repeat track 1, so there would be music there for her all night. Then I switched off the light and went downstairs, to see how A was.

My plan had been to bring the twins together when B's injuries had healed. I was hoping for a fairly speedy recovery, in physical terms – I had expected to reunite them after about a week – but B made no real progress that I could detect. She would not eat. She rarely moved. Sometimes she seemed to be sleeping, sometimes her eyes were open, but I had no idea what she was experiencing, whether she was in pain, whether she had the will to get better. I knew that was the key to her recovery. If she wanted to live, she would – and yet, from the very start, I felt she had sustained too great an insult to the system to survive. It wasn't so much that she had lost some blood, or experienced the usual trauma – I couldn't fully put it into words, but there had been a moment, just as I was concluding the operation, when I had become aware of the spaces inside the body, how the tissue isn't as tightly packed as I had imagined, how there are small, vital gaps everywhere. I had been aware of this in animals, but for some reason, I hadn't been prepared for that in a human body. Yet it was those spaces that seemed important, as I stitched B up and dressed the wound; it was those spaces that seemed most vulnerable, most sensitive. That tiny space in the larynx, that space I had violated, would never be the same again, and I think B knew that, at some level. I could have waited for a full recovery, but I was afraid she would simply give up, and I wanted to see what happened, when I brought the twins together.

So it was that, two days later, I carried B into the basement room and set her down in the pen next to her brother. Neither child made a sound. I waited several minutes, but it was evident that they had no intention of attempting to communicate while I was there. They didn't even move: they sat side by side in the pen, gazing at one another, waiting for me to go. The expression on their faces was identical: a look of infinite grief, a profound hurt that seemed to affect A at least as much, perhaps more than B. I stepped outside and locked the door behind me. By the time I reached the observation window, they had already moved together, and were holding on to one another, rocking slightly, the way monkeys do when they are hurt or frightened. I watched for a while, then I withdrew. At that moment, I knew for certain that it was hopeless to continue. By performing the laryngotomy on B, I had damaged both twins irreparably. The resilience I had taken for granted in B had been illusory. I didn't know if it was the operation, or the brief, yet for them, interminable period of separation that had broken their spirit, but all I had left were two injured children, turned in upon their own special world, from which I was exiled forever.

I spent the afternoon working in the garden. It was still warm, and the borders were in bloom. I pottered about for some time, dead-heading the roses, pulling up weeds. For the first time, I allowed myself to fully recognise that the experiment had failed. There was no way of deciding whether the twins' singing was a language in itself, or whether they were simply singing for the fun of it. Perhaps their song really had been nothing more than a celebration of their own being, their likeness, the sense they had of themselves and of one another. Perhaps it was the running commentary of two perplexed souls, unable to make any sense of their world, but delighting in it, nevertheless. All of a sudden it occurred to me that they had existed all their lives in a state, not of innocence, but of grace – which is to say, awareness, playfulness in the purest sense, a special mix of detachment and interest that made them appear, at times, superior to me in their manner of being in the world. That was it. These children, singing to one another in the confines of a blank laboratory room, possessed something I could not begin to imagine. They had passed beyond the limits of my language and ended up beyond my control, outside the scope, even, of my observation. It was a sobering thought. Nevertheless, there were lessons to be learned. Next time, I told myself, I would set things up differently. I would obtain a new child and keep it in total isolation. It would be a simple matter to find another homeless woman. I could start again. In the meantime, I would make the best of a bad job with the twins. It was evident that A would not sing any longer: he must have known that B could not reply. In other words, there was an imbalance between them. If that imbalance were righted, there was a chance that they might attempt to find some new way of communicating. Perhaps I had allowed them to rely on their singing for too long, and they would be unable to find an alternative. Still, it was worth a try. I would perform one more laryngotomy and, if that failed, I would scrap the experiment and start again.

The second operation was as successful as the first. I found it pleasurable, once again, to linger over the tiny gaps, to see the intricacy and beauty of the flesh in close detail. However, A's response on recovery was even worse than B's. He was more listless – less willing, I think, to recover. He developed a fever, and symptoms of infection which, with no worthwhile antibiotics, there was little I could have done to combat. I placed him back in the pen with his sister, and they lay together, gazing at one another, disconsolate, spent. I was relieved, in a way, to be spared their constant singing, but I now understood that I would have to take steps to close this experiment down and make ready for another. Perhaps I felt guilty, too, for taking things so far; either way, I could no longer bear to have them in the house. The experiment was over: it had ended in failure, more or less, and the twins were a constant reminder of how badly it had gone. Besides, it was obvious that they were unhappy, and I realised that it would be a mercy to simply end their lives. I had already sketched out my plans, working out a strategy for finding a new homeless woman, deciding where I would keep her, thinking through all the possibilities. I would have to be careful, but once I had found an appropriate person, once I had managed to get her back to the house, I could keep her in the basement, out of sight and mind. I thought of the girls I had seen in London, hopeless, desperate for food and shelter and a sense of safety. They soon became suspicious and self-aware after a few months on the streets, but how easy it would be to find a young runaway on her first or second night: someone inexperienced, someone vulnerable. I'd read about men who wandered around the stations and backstreets at night, hunting down such girls. If they could do it, I could. How much better for the girl if I found her, rather than someone like Jimmy. Even if she wasn't a willing partner, even if she didn't understand what was happening, or what her true purpose was, she would be comfortable and well looked after, for a time at least. Most importantly, she would be engaged in something worthwhile.

Meanwhile, I had to be rid of the twins. I considered several methods of disposal. Drowning occurred to me, but I dismissed it as involving too much direct contact with the children. The truth was, I felt squeamish. The same problem arose with smothering or asphyxiation. I had a good supply of valium and a variety of drugs Mother had been prescribed over the course of her illness, but I felt they might be useful in my attempts to procure a homeless woman. Other possibilities included alcohol and carbon monoxide poisoning, or the simple withdrawal of food and drink. In the end, however, I lighted upon the perfect answer.

I had forgotten that every garden is an apothecary's shop. It contains narcotics, emetics, astringents, love potions, hallucinogens. A few years before I had begun the experiment with the twins, I had studied the effects of plant substances, especially hallucinogens and poisons. Now it all came back to me: the effects of yew and cherry laurel, laburnum, deadly nightshade, bryony, various fungi. It pleased me to think that the most powerful drugs could be found within a mile's walk of any home, especially in autumn, when the woods are full of toadstools. Every park, every stretch of waste ground, every local woodland offered the kinds of plants that could destroy a man's inner organs in a matter of days, or tear his mind open in a few hours. I had read of cases where children had swallowed only a few berries of *Atropa belladonna*, the deadly nightshade, and had begun to hallucinate vividly, the hallucinations becoming more and more intense as the poison worked, until finally they died – not from the poison that cause the visions, but from another, quite distinct substance. During my earlier researches, I had prepared several extracts of these substances: atropa, foxglove, monkshood, without really knowing what I intended to do with them. Now, all of a sudden, I had my answer.

I was working at the far end of the garden, by the wall, where Mother had trained a pillar of Albertine up a trellis. I was enjoying the scent, the warmth of the afternoon sun, the quiet of the place. The singing in my ears had stopped and, for the first time in months, I was at peace. I'm not sure when, but it was some time in the long heat of the afternoon, the way it sometimes happens, when you've been outside, in a closed space, alone for a while. I had my back to the house and, all of a sudden, I felt someone was there, standing at the door, watching me. I turned around quickly. It sounds absurd, but I half-expected to see Mother there, standing at the door, calling me to come in for some tea. I could see her in my mind's eye, in her blue and red summer dress and her straw hat. She was as beautiful as ever. But when I looked, nobody was there. I saw nothing but the holly trees by the path, the back door, the study window. The sensation only lasted a moment, but it was beguiling, as if I'd been touched, like one of the children in the books Mother used to read me, by the cool hand of some otherworldly presence. It didn't occur to me that my intruder of two years before had returned: after all, how could he? He was long dead, I thought.

Nevertheless, when I reached the house, the evidence that someone had been there was undeniable. He must have been watching me for some time. It reminded me of the time before, when I'd found Jimmy's traces in the garden, but it was a ridiculously long time before I actually realised that this was the same individual who had come before, the same all-seeing person, returning to haunt me. In other words, I had killed Jimmy for nothing. That would have explained his behaviour in the churchyard. Now, I suddenly realised, I would have to put all my plans on hold. I would have to delay finding a girl, I would have to get rid of the twins quickly, and clear the basement, in case anyone came prowling. Worst of all, if my intruder returned, I would have to go through the process I had gone through with Jimmy, with its attendant risks, all over again.

That evening, I bought the local paper. It wasn't something I usually did; I suppose I wanted to check to see if anything out of the ordinary had happened, if there was some new information about Jimmy's death, or Lillian's disappearance, or some new evidence that had come to light. I flicked through quickly, looking for anything that might indicate cause for concern, but, to be honest, I was hardly aware of what I was reading. It all seemed so absurd, that mixture of road traffic accidents and advertisements for bridal wear, of births and deaths and recipes for lemon meringue pie. I'm not even sure, looking back, if I was conscious of having noticed the feature story on the cover, but I suppose I must have done. When I began reading, it was the picture that first caught my attention. I recognised Jeremy Olerud right away, though he looked clean and tidy, in a collar and tie, with his shock of yellow hair brushed back, and he looked different – less enraged, almost happy. The story was rather thin. It said the boy had been found drowned in the boating lake at Weston Park. The local police were asking for anyone who had seen the child, or who might have any information about the circumstances of his death, to come forward. It was obvious that they suspected foul play. The story went on to say that Karen Olerud, the mother of the drowned boy, had gone missing in mysterious circumstances. The police were appealing to anyone who knew her whereabouts to come forward. I was surprised at the amateurish quality of the writing, even for a local newspaper. They actually used terms like *mysterious circumstances*. The report concluded with a summary of Jeremy's school career and behavioural problems.

In my garden, the seasons don't just begin and end. Traces of winter remain, far into April and May, films and threads of moisture and blackness, small pockets of leaf mould and frost in the raked leaves behind the shed and in the shady corners of the north wall, where it never really gets warm. Autumn arrives a degree at a time: a flower head tilts and collapses into a mass of inky tissue, a few leaves drift from the pear trees on the wall, an apple ripens too soon, and falls unnoticed. Winter begins with the chrysanthemums. It had taken me years to notice these things. As a child, I had gone to bed in summer and wakened next morning to windows shot with frost and the smell of apples in the kitchen. Spring was one sudden narcissus. The only subtleties I had ever understood were those Mother had pointed out; even then, I made no connections, I took everything at face value.

Now, after my months with the twins, I felt different. Sometimes it was as if every detail was too exquisite to bear: a single petal drifting across the lawn, a single drop of rain suspended on a twig, the first flakes of snow that fell out of a blue-black sky – everything was present. At the same time, I felt completely attuned to my surroundings. Every change in the light, every new sound, every change registered with me at a purely physical level. One evening, only days after I had decided to kill the twins, I was standing at the side door, in a dark place I usually only passed through, where nothing grew but ivy and periwinkle. The side wall was about ten feet high and close to the house; there was a door through to the garage that I always kept locked, and a narrow path that ran to the back wall, past the shed and the compost bins. I had always thought this was where my intruder had entered, clambering over the garage roof and tumbling in over this wall: it had never occurred to me that he might come across the fields, ford the little stream and slip in through the back gate, which I would normally have kept locked, but occasionally forgot. I suppose I was standing out there that night in the hope of catching him. I know I was listening, watching. Then, as I caught the first hint of autumn in the air, the merest hint of water and caramel, I realised someone else was there, just around the corner of the house, quite close, all tension, as aware, suddenly, of me, as I was of him. I don't know how I knew it, or how I knew it was a person, not an animal, but I was quite certain my visitor had returned. I ought to have been more careful. It might have been one of Jimmy's friends, or some common burglar – whoever it was, he might have been armed. Yet, before I had thought it through, I walked quickly to the back of the house and turned the corner. Perhaps I expected the prowler to hear me coming and make a run for it; instead, I found myself face to face with Karen Olerud.

She was standing by the honeysuckle Mother had trained along wires at the back of the house, as if she had stopped, casually, on her regular evening stroll around the garden, to inhale its deep, sweet fragrance. Her hair was dishevelled, and stuck here and there with dried leaves, and I noticed there were scratches and streaks of mud on her face and neck – it was as if she had come through a wilderness to find me. I suppose I should have been surprised to see her, but I wasn't. I was glad. I understood immediately that she had been my mysterious visitor all those months before. She was the one who had left that trail of soft, black footprints in the snow, the one who had become a ghost in order to haunt me, appearing and melting away, staining everything she touched with shadows and dust. She had been a silent witness to my life with Lillian. She must have seen us at the window; she must have watched us, on those nights when I undressed the girl and led her away; she had stood in silence, perhaps for hours at a time, while Lillian moved from room to room, making breakfast, bringing me tea, fetching books from the library, watching television. Perhaps it disturbed her, to think I had chosen this child in her place. She would have thought of me as a lover, no matter what I had done. Suddenly, everything was clear: she had never meant to threaten or intimidate us. I had killed Jimmy for nothing. All she had done to call attention to her vigil had been nothing other than cries for attention, desperate attempts to let me know she still wanted me.

I felt elated. The story from the previous day's paper ran through my mind and I knew – I knew for certain – what it had deliberately left untold. Karen Olerud had killed her son. She had drowned him deliberately, and now she had come to me, because she was free, and she had nowhere else to go. I no longer had any need to acquire a homeless woman. I had the perfect subject, someone who needed me more than I needed her, someone I knew could be easily managed. All I had to do was take her in.

'Hello, Karen,' I said.

She gazed at me as if she wasn't quite sure I was real.

'You look tired,' I said, but that wasn't the whole truth. She looked beautiful, standing there, in the fading light, and I remembered her body with a sudden rush of desire – the smoothness of her skin, the warmth of her mouth, how wet she had been when I first touched her. I was also intrigued by the idea that, for the first time, her mask would have to be discarded; that, from now on, I would no longer be obliged to play her game. If I took her in, I would have her on my terms and I think she knew that.

'Do you want to come in?' I continued.

She didn't reply. For a moment I wondered if she had lost her mind: she seemed so dazed, so out of touch with reality. Yet I knew she had recognised me. It occurred to me that she had spent all her energy on getting as far as my house and, now that she had arrived, she could barely function. She was only waiting to see what I would do.

I took hold of her arm, gently.

'Why don't you come in and rest for a while,' I said.

I led her inside and she followed me through the house in a daze of gratitude. I helped her out of her wet dress in the bathroom, then I ran a hot bath and told her to finish getting undressed. For a moment she seemed confused, as if she thought I wanted to have sex with her then and there, as the steam rose and clouded the windows, and, when I understood what she was thinking, I have to admit I was tempted. There was something about her, as she stood before me, streaked with mud, with the bruise on her mouth and the cuts and scratches on her arms and face, something that excited me, and I had to collect myself and tell her, gently, that she would feel better after a nice hot bath. The look of gratitude returned to her face and she lowered herself into the hot water and sat waiting, as if she expected me to bathe her. I told her to get cleaned up, then I picked up her dirty clothes and took them away. When I returned, with an old dressing gown of Mother's, she was still sitting there, helpless, stunned, lost in her own world. I began to wash her then, wiping away the mud, rinsing the blood and dirt from her hair, bathing her cuts and bruises with warm water. I felt an unexpected tenderness for her, all of a sudden. She had come to me just when I needed her, as if she had known all along what was required. When she was clean, I helped her out of the bath and dried her gently, then I draped the dressing gown around her shoulders and led her across the landing to Mother's room. Nobody else had been allowed into that space since Mother had died; for the first time, I understood why I had kept it intact, just as she had left it, five years before. Karen was exactly Mother's size: the night-dress I chose for her was an exact fit. I gave her two of Mother's old pills, so she would sleep soundly through the coming hours, then I kissed her briefly on the mouth and, telling her to get some sleep, I lowered her into the bed and pulled the covers up around her shoulders. When I made as if to leave, she caught hold of me and clung to my arms like a frightened child, and I had to reassure her, stroking her hair, kissing her face, telling her everything was going to be all right. After a while, she let me slip free.

'Go to sleep,' I said. 'Everything's fine. I'll see you in the morning.'

I waited a few minutes, till I was sure she was asleep. Then I locked her into Mother's room and went downstairs to prepare the final meal for the twins. I had to work quickly – and I am aware that, in my haste, I took risks I ought not to have taken. I might have been seen; Karen might have wakened and panicked. Yet I didn't care about any of that. I didn't even think of it. I felt utterly confident. It was like the feeling gamblers have, when they know they cannot lose. I was elated, I suppose, that I was about to begin the experiment again. I served the meal, feeding the twins by hand, as they were unable to feed themselves, then I went upstairs to make coffee. Later, I went down to the basement and, in spite of my old fear that they were still alive somehow, still waiting to catch me out, I retrieved their cooling bodies and carried them out into the garden. Strange, how empty their faces looked out of doors. While Karen slept, I laid the children next to their mother, in the iris garden, turning the bodies so they lay face to face in the wet earth.

It is remarkable how little Karen has changed, how beautiful she still is, in spite of the scratches and bruises. It's over three years since I last slept with her, but I calculate that she must still be in her mid-thirties, still capable of having another child, perhaps more. I realise now that I have wanted her, while we have been apart; now that she is here, I feel certain that I can manage the situation. The essential thing will be to make sure she doesn't become independent enough to question what is happening when I take the children away, but I know, if she becomes difficult, it will be easy enough to dispose of her. Nobody knows where she is. If I had to kill her, I could bury her in the garden, next to Lillian and the twins, and return to the earlier plan of finding another homeless girl. Not that I even imagine it will come to that. I am quite sure I can keep her content; with simple displays of kindness and a regular supply of alcohol, she will accept everything I say and do. Besides, I am fond of her, in my way. It felt good, when I kissed her on the forehead and turned off the lights, knowing I would return later to the warmth of her bruised skin; it feels good, now, to have a woman in the house again. A few hours ago, when I left her in Mother's room, locking the door carefully behind me, I experienced a sudden thrill of joy, as if I were locking away some hidden treasure that I'd been waiting years to find, the one thing I had never expected: a necessary gift, an indisputable moment of divine grace.